Liberating Mrs. McGraw

Captive Western Widows

Cheryl Wright

Copyright

Liberating Mrs. McGraw

(Captive Western Widows)

Copyright ©2024 by Cheryl Wright

Small Town Romance Publications

Editing: Sarah Lamb Editing

ALL RIGHTS RESERVED

Dedication

To Margaret Tanner, my very dear friend and fellow author, for her enduring encouragement and friendship.

To Alan, my husband of over forty-nine years, who has been a relentless supporter of my writing and dreams for many years.

To You, my wonderful readers, who encourage me to continue writing these stories. It is such a joy knowing so many of you enjoy reading my stories as much as I love writing them for you.

Table of Contents

Chapter One

Pleasant Valley, Montana, 1880s

Maisy McGraw grimaced as she shimmied down the wooden column.

With each movement, Maisy felt every splinter of wood. Even despite the heavy black gown she wore.

She wasn't sure how long she'd been held captive, but believed it to be a few days at least. Otis Doss had tried everything short of torture to make her sign. She resisted the urge to rub her wrists where the ropes had cut into her delicate skin.

Despite the urgency to get away, she took her time, not wanting to risk a fall from the second-floor roof. She said a silent prayer of thanks for the porch column. Without it, she would have no means of escape. Her mind was fuzzy. Did that mean her captor had drugged her? It must be the reason she'd not tried the window as a means of escape before this.

She was a strong, independent woman. Callum always told her so. Maisy felt empty—she'd been that way since her husband had died suddenly. It made her wonder why she hadn't just let Otis have his way. She could wipe her hands of the entire situation. Perhaps even leave town.

Except she knew Callum would not want her to be left destitute. A small sob escaped her lips as she thought of what she'd lost. Money meant little to Maisy, but her husband was her entire world. And now he was gone.

Interrupting her thoughts, two hands grabbed her waist. Maisy let out her breath at the impact, and her heart pounded so hard she felt lightheaded. How did Otis get to her so quickly? Perhaps he'd seen her through a window? No matter now, she had to save herself, and the only way she knew how to do that was to scream.

Opening her mouth wide, Maisy breathed deeply, ready to scream far louder than she ever had before. Except a large hand covered her mouth before any sound could come out. She struggled, but he was far too strong. She kicked at Otis's legs as he lifted and carried her. If she couldn't scream, Maisy would ensure she did the most damage she could.

But now she was confused. Otis was a runt. He didn't have the strength to lift the cash drawers, let alone carry a woman taller than himself. No matter, she couldn't worry about that now. He had obviously sent someone else to do his dirty work.

Once he had her sign everything over, Maisy knew what her fate would be. Otis would kill her. That way, Maisy could not go to the authorities. Regardless of her actions, Maisy knew she was doomed.

As she was dragged into an unfamiliar room, her heart continued to pound. Where was she? This was it. By Maisy's reckoning, she only had minutes left. It was the only way he would get her husband's business. Of course Otis wanted the bank. He was nothing more than a filthy polecat. A greedy one at that.

Callum had paid him handsomely, but it wasn't enough for Otis. He had to have it all.

Her mind still reeling, Maisy continued kicking. With her mouth still firmly covered, Maisy was guided toward a seat. "If you promise not to scream, I'll take my hand away."

This voice did not belong to Otis Doss. Glancing up confirmed it. Her heart still pounded as loudly as before. Why she expected it to slow, Maisy did not know. Except that she couldn't be certain the danger was over. "Who…who are you?" she whispered. The stranger stood tall above her. Her eyes grazed him from head to toe. He grinned. Then reached out a hand. It was then it hit her. "I suppose Otis sent you to grab me again." It was a statement, not a question, and she sighed so loud they could have heard it out on the main street.

He was big as a bear, and Maisy shuddered. Otis was no gentleman, and he had the body to match. Was this his way of proving his masculinity? It wasn't working.

"Beau Hardner," he said as he studied her. Then appeared confused. "Otis? I don't know anyone named Otis. I saw you falling down…"

"Falling? I wasn't falling?" she near screeched. "I was escaping! At least I was until you came along."

She raked him with her eyes again, only this time he didn't laugh. Her words had him reeling backwards. "Escaping?" he asked as he pushed his hat back and scratched his head. "Ma'am, I have no idea what you're talking about."

Relief filled her, and Maisy felt tears fill her eyes. She blinked them back. "You…you don't? Otis didn't send you?" Her tears fell unbidden, and Maisy wiped them away.

The man standing before her scowled, then sat down beside her. "Ma'am," he said.

"Maisy. Maisy McGraw," she told him cautiously.

"Mrs. McGraw," he said, repeating her name. "You'd better start from the beginning."

Chapter Two

Mrs. McGraw stared at him. He totally understood—she didn't know him, and yet, Beau was asking the widow to trust him explicitly.

"I…" She stumbled on that one word, and Beau knew he had to put her at ease. He reached out and covered her hand with his.

"I am here to help," he told her gently. "It's what I do for a living." She stared down at their entwined hands and glared. Beau snatched his hand away.

"How do I know if I can trust you? I thought Otis was trustworthy, so did Callum." Her bottom lip quivered and Beau knew he needed to hear the entire story.

"Ma'am, Mrs. McGraw," he said. "You can trust me. I spent several years working as a marshal. Now I work for myself."

Her features seemed to soften somewhat, but Beau could tell she was still on edge. "Why haven't I seen you before?" she demanded. It was a fair question.

"I've only recently moved to town. Now," he said firmly. "Tell me about this man Otis." Beau listened carefully to Maisy McGraw. He seethed as the story unfolded. When he learned about Otis Doss, assistant to the bank manager who was Maisy's husband, anger filled him. When her husband died suddenly and mysteriously, Otis took it upon himself to take over.

He listened carefully to every word she spoke. Beau was surprised Maisy was able to keep her emotions in check, and didn't want to prolong her agony. "How long since you've eaten?" he asked, when she finally finished relaying her dreadful ordeal. Changing the subject so abruptly might take her mind off her dire situation.

"What day is it?" she asked, confusion in her voice.

He stared at her. "Thursday," Beau told her, and this time her expression was one of shock.

"Thursday? Otis grabbed me on…Monday. Or perhaps it was Tuesday." She shook her head then, and Beau knew the widow had been drugged. Her confusion over the past days was far too pronounced for her not to have been.

"I need you to come with me to the doctor's office. To make sure you're in good health." This time, she stared at him in utter confusion. He reached for her hands and pulled Maisy to her feet. Then they made their way to the doctor's office.

Beau wondered what he was walking into, but didn't care. This woman was bewildered and in imminent danger. She needed protection. Beau knew he was the right person for the job.

~*~

"Apart from some large splinters, Mrs. McGraw is in good health," Doctor Peter Murphy told Beau. "I am certain she was drugged at some point, but there's no way to tell with what."

Fury burned through Beau. "Laudanum?" he guessed. It was what most of the criminals used. Mostly because it was easy to get, with no questions asked.

"I believe so," the doctor said. "I've cleaned and dressed the wounds from the wood splinters. What's going to happen now?" he asked, curiosity seeming to get the better of him.

"I'll protect her and ensure this Otis person sees justice." Beau knew that could be harder than it sounded, but Maisy McGraw needed his help.

They bid goodbye to Doctor Murphy and left his rooms. "What now?" Maisy asked. He glanced down at her, and to Beau, she appeared vulnerable. Perhaps because she was. She brushed a lock of hair back from her face, and for the first time he noticed how truly disheveled she appeared. Until this moment, he was far more concerned about her safety and her health to even consider the way she looked.

"I should take you home," he said firmly. "You can clean up and change into fresh clothes." The moment the words were out of his mouth, Beau realized it sounded as though she was a complete mess. "I didn't mean…" he began, but she waved a hand in front of herself as though brushing away his words.

Then she glanced down at her gown. "You're right, I am a mess," she said, sounding more resigned than she had since the moment they met. She brushed back that loose lock again, and guilt filled him. Why had he said anything? Now she felt bad, and that wasn't his intention.

He stopped walking and turned to face her. "You are not a mess," he said firmly. "You are beautiful, despite what you've been through. All because of that awful man your husband trusted." He swore under his breath then, and she stared at him in horror. "I apologize. But a man can't help feeling that way about another who has done something like this."

Her features softened, and she relaxed a little. "Which way to your home?" he asked, and she pointed. It was easy to see, even from the center of town. It was the largest building by far and stood out amongst the smaller buildings that surrounded Pleasant Valley. He flinched. It wasn't that he didn't want to go there, but it reminded him of the utter indulgence of the wealthy. If only they got to see the destitute, things might change. Although Beau decided the distance between the rich and the poor would never lessen.

When he glanced down, she was staring at him. "I know what you're thinking," she said. "It is truly atrocious. I begged Callum not to make me live there, to find something smaller, but he had to prove himself to this town." She scowled then, as though remembering a side to her husband she'd rather forget. "He'd been living in that monstrosity for over a year when I married him." She sighed then, and it told Beau more than her words ever could.

Beau lifted both hands in front of himself. "No judgement," he said firmly. "How folks live is not my business. Nor should it be."

The closer they got, the more formidable the building seemed. It made Beau wonder how anyone could live there.

They walked up to the front door. It was then Maisy seemed confused. "My reticule," she said. "Where is my reticule? I need my keys."

"You didn't have one with you," Beau told her. "I can break in, if that's what you want," then waited for her decision.

Maisy McGraw closed her eyes and shook her head slightly. If he hadn't been staring at her, he wouldn't have even seen it. "I…" She opened her eyes.

"There's a hidden key." She closed her eyes again, and Beau instinctively understood she was trying to recall its whereabouts.

He hoped and prayed the keys weren't hidden in a flower pot. It was the most common place for keys to be concealed.

She opened her eyes abruptly, then headed toward a low hanging branch on a nearby tree. "I can't reach," she said quietly, "but I believe it's hidden in that abandoned bird's nest."

Beau followed her to the tree and reached for the nest. The key was nowhere to be found.

"It's deep into the nest," Mrs. McGraw said. "Try not to destroy it. It's a good hiding place. Callum placed it there soon after we married. It hasn't been needed until now." Her face seemed to collapse as she mentioned her dead husband. He hadn't been gone long, from what she'd said, and now she found herself in this terrible situation.

"I will do my best," Beau said, then moments later was able to retrieve the key. "Ah, here it is, and you can't see where it's been retrieved." That put a tentative smile on her face, which lifted Beau's spirits. It was clear Mrs. McGraw had been through a lot lately. Far more than any woman should be expected to endure.

He headed toward the front door, and she followed. The key was a little tight in the lock, but he persisted until the door let go and allowed them entry. "Ladies first," Beau said, then glanced behind them. Once he was convinced they weren't followed, he closed the door, ensuring it was locked.

The last thing they needed was uninvited guests. One in particular.

"Do you mind if I call you Maisy?" he asked, as she motioned for him to sit down in the sitting room. Or was it the parlor? The house was as grand on the inside as it was on the outside. "Have you been staying here alone?" he asked as he sat in one of the comfortable chairs. No doubt that single chair cost more money than he made in a year.

"Please do call me Maisy," she said, then visibly shuddered. "I was staying here alone, but it wasn't easy. Every sound, every creak of the walls, all echoed throughout the building. A few weeks ago, I decided to move into the hotel until I felt comfortable returning home."

"He waited until you felt at ease with your surroundings. And then he swooped in and snatched you." It would have been difficult to gain entry here, even more so if they had staff. Having walked from the center of town to the stately home, Beau knew there was no way to conceal any attempt to drag an unwilling woman back into town.

She sat down on the sofa, not far from where Beau was, and glanced down at her hands that now rested in her lap. "I made it easy for him, didn't I?"

"All of this is on Otis Doss. You can't blame yourself for his actions." He stood then, and moved to sit beside the widow. "Where did it happen? I only ask, as I'm trying to determine if anyone saw what happened."

She shook her head daintily. "Otis visited my hotel room, and asked if we could have tea together. He wanted to go over some figures, he said. It's the last thing I recall."

Beau breathed in, then let it out slowly. "He drugged you," he said firmly. "What was the arrangement? Did Otis take over the bank, or were you doing that?" He was certain he knew the answer, but had to ask anyway.

"Did I run the…?" She almost laughed, except it was no laughing matter. "I have no idea about accounting, or banks, or anything. I left Otis to do whatever was necessary."

Things were becoming clearer by the minute. "Do you have a copy of your late husband's will?" Beau asked. "I need to check something."

She stood, then hurried toward what Beau assumed was Callum McGraw's study. He caught up quickly and followed her in. Maisy went to a large painting that sat behind the large mahogany desk, which took up a big part of the room. He hurried forward to help as she tried to lift the heavy painting from the wall. Once placed against the wall, he stared at the safe that was previously obscured.

"I truly hope you have the combination," he said. If not, surely the McGraw's lawyer would have a copy? It could prove crucial to a case against Otis. Or it might simply explain the man's actions.

"I do," she said quietly. "I only hope I recall it correctly." She began to turn the circular lock, holding her breath with each turn of the dial. She leaned in on the last turn, and Beau heard the quiet click.

Maisy reached in and on finding the will, handed it to him. "I haven't read it," she said softly. "I've had too much to deal with. I told Otis to continue at the bank as normal." She closed her eyes and shook her head then. "He was my husband's assistant and had been for a couple of years, I believe. Long before he and I married. Callum trusted him explicitly."

That had been a mistake, but Beau didn't voice his opinion. "Do you mind if I take this to the sitting room and read it?"

"Go ahead while I tidy up," she said. Maisy locked the safe again and hurried away.

Beau was keen to read the conditions of the will. With no children to pass the bank to, Beau was more than a little interested to know exactly who benefited from Callum McGraw's death.

Chapter Three

Standing in front of the large decorative mirror in the luxurious bathroom, Maisy could see why Beau suggested she clean up. She really was a mess.

Not that she should be surprised—not when she'd been drugged and locked up for days. Otis had tried time and again to force her to sign over the deed to the bank. Maisy was having none of it. Callum might have inherited his early fortune, but he'd worked hard to earn what they had now, and she would not hand it over to the likes of Otis Doss. A man she now knew to be nothing more than a thug.

How Callum had trusted that man, Maisy would never know. She'd only known Otis since her marriage to Callum, but she'd always felt uneasy around him. She wasn't sure what it was about the man, but he made her feel uncomfortable.

When she mentioned it to Callum, he laughed her fears aside. Maisy now knew she had good reason to worry about him. She stepped out of her now ruined gown and washed herself thoroughly.

This was the result of three days of being held against her will, perhaps four. Maisy shook her head. Otis had been determined, but Maisy knew she couldn't hold out forever. In the beginning, she was tied to the bed in her own hotel room.

She glanced down at her wrists. Red marks were still prominent there.

He poured water down her throat until she choked, but she still didn't give in. Eventually he removed the fastenings, realizing it did nothing except make her angry.

The moment he left the last time, she sprung into action. With no fastenings on her hands or legs, it was her one chance to get away.

Maisy shook her head. She didn't want to remember the horror of it all, and instead, continued to bathe until she'd cleaned the pungent odor of Otis Doss from her skin.

She then smothered herself in rose water, assuring there was nothing of that awful man left on her body. Maisy then dressed in fresh clothes and attended to her hair. It was a dreadful mess.

When she stared in the mirror again, she saw the old Maisy standing there, except she knew the woman she had seen each and every day in that beautiful ornate mirror would never be the same person again.

Her eyes filled with tears at all she had lost, including her husband, but she refused to allow them to fall. She took the face cloth and plunged it into cold water, then held it to her eyes. The last thing she wanted was to show weakness. It was the one thing she believed had saved her from her abductor.

The vile creature could not understand how she'd held out so long, but she was strong. Maisy would never give in to a man like that.

Finally, she was ready to face Beau Hardner, and learn what he'd discovered in her husband's will. Whatever it was, she now believed it had put her life in danger.

~*~

Beau glanced up as she entered the sitting room. "Oh!" she said. "I apologize, I should have offered you coffee." Except she hadn't been there for days, which meant the woodstove had no fire, and the kettle had no water.

He said nothing, but smiled. "I don't need coffee, but thank you," he said, then went back to reading the will held in his hands. "Your husband really did trust that man, didn't he?" Beau pierced her with his gaze.

Concern filled her. What was in her husband's will?

He indicated for her to sit down. Maisy did as he asked. Then she braced herself for what was to come.

"According to your husband's will, the bank belongs to you."

She breathed a sigh of relief. There was nothing untoward there. Nothing that would cause Otis to kidnap her.

"However, and this is the important part," he said firmly. "Upon your death, the bank goes to Otis Doss, his trusted assistant."

Maisy gasped. "How…how could Callum do that to me? He…" Tears fell down her cheeks. As determined as she'd been, Maisy now understood her life really was in danger. "He's put me in a precarious situation." With her head in her hands, Maisy sobbed. Was it any wonder Otis tried to get her to sign over the bank to him? Callum must have told him about the will, and Otis's greed got the better of him.

Beau reached over and held her hand. "You need to consult a lawyer, but first we need to secure both your home and the bank." Maisy stared at him. "The last thing you want is Otis having full rein of the bank's books. Not that I believe he'll return after what he did, but you never can tell with his sort."

Maisy shook her head in disbelief. What she would do now, she did not know. It was clear she couldn't return to her hotel room. It was where Otis had snatched her to begin with. And where her nightmare began. Beau patted her hand. It was obvious he was trying to console her, but Maisy needed much more than consoling. "I need you to work for me," she said suddenly.

He stared at her. "I didn't do all this for you to employ me. It was done in my service as a good Christian." Beau handed the will back to her. "Lock this up for now. Do you feel up to going back to the bank?"

Sympathy covered his face, but that wasn't what she wanted. "Whether you asked for the job or not, you've already proven your worth." She stood then and headed back into her husband's study where she again opened the safe. She heard Beau behind her. After placing the will back where it belonged, she turned to face him. "Take this as a down payment," she said, handing him a large wad of banknotes. "Secure whatever staff you require—I need to be safe, and so does my husband's bank."

"It's far too much," Beau said.

Maisy stared at him. "It's only money," she told him. "Otis needs to be taken to account for what he did. I need your help, and I insist you accept this down payment."

Beau reached out and took the money. He placed it in his jacket pocket where it couldn't be seen. "This will certainly go a long way toward protection for you," he said.

As Maisy locked the safe again, she realized without Beau Hardner seeing her climbing down from the second-floor window, she may have been in a far worse condition than she was. She may also have been caught again. Otis Doss would surely know by now she was gone.

Would the snake show his face at the bank again? Surely not. Then again, he had no idea Maisy now had a private bodyguard. Someone who would be by her side every moment. Not to mention the other guards Beau would secure to keep her safe.

It was the last thing she wanted, but it was blatantly clear she was no longer safe while Otis was on the loose.

He needed to be brought to justice, and she hoped Beau and his team were able to make that happen.

Chapter Four

Beau accompanied his new client to the bank. Her bank—it was legally hers, and he was there to ensure it stayed that way.

They walked side by side into the double-story building, and Maisy introduced him to the few staff who worked there. Then they went upstairs to the manager's office. As they reached the top of the stairs, Maisy paused.

He heard her gasp, then chaos ensued.

"It's Otis," she said, urgently pointing to the man sitting behind the desk of the bank manager's office.

Otis Doss glanced up, saw the pair standing there, and ran faster than a rabbit running for its life. Beau ran toward him, but he wasn't quick enough. The vile creature got away. Beau chased him down the stairs, but not before Otis had shoved Maisy aside.

He wanted to catch the polecat so badly, but he needed to check on Maisy who lay unmoving to the side of the stairs.

"Maisy," he said as he shook her gently. He stared down into her face. She was pale, but appeared to be breathing. Beau turned when he heard someone on the stairs. If it was Otis, he wouldn't know what hit him. Beau reached for his gun—which is what he should have done earlier.

"Wait, I work here," the male voice told him hurriedly. "What's going on?" he asked, concern all over his face.

"Otis Doss is trying to kill Mrs. McGraw. Has he left the building?" Beau asked. When the man nodded, he barked out orders. "Lock the front door. I'll be down shortly," he demanded, then turned back to Maisy who was finally coming around, much to Beau's relief.

"Yes, Sir," the young man said quickly, then disappeared. Beau heard the click of the front door, and was even more relieved.

"What happened?" Maisy asked as he stared down into her ashen face. She glanced around, trying to place her surroundings. "Otis?" she finally said.

"He's gone. I doubt he'll be back, but with someone like that, you never can know." Beau was fuming. If only he'd caught the man, Otis would be rotting in a jail cell right now.

Maisy tried to get to her feet, but began to sway. "I'm fine," she said, brushing his hands away. It was becoming very clear that Maisy McGraw was an independent woman. She was not going to be pleased with the plan Beau had worked out to keep her safe.

He guided her to a chair in the manager's office, then went behind the bank manager's desk to see what Otis had been involved in when they arrived. It only took moments to know he was working his way through the ledgers. No doubt ensuring the bank still had plenty of money for him to steal.

Only it wasn't going to happen. "Don't touch anything here," he told Maisy, then went to her side. "How are you feeling now?"

"Much better," she said.

The large bruise on the side of her face said otherwise.

~*~

Sheriff Tommy Garrett pounded on the bank's door. He peered through the window as Beau headed his way. "Sheriff," Beau said as he shook the man's hand. "Thank you for coming so quickly."

"Sounded urgent," the sheriff said, glancing about. "I heard Mrs. McGraw was assaulted. Should we send for the doc?"

"She has a nasty bruise on the side of her face. This isn't the first time she's been attacked by Otis Doss." Beau studied the sheriff for his reaction. As he suspected, the lawman was surprised at the revelation.

"What's he been up to? It's not like Otis."

Beau stopped himself from groaning out loud. It seemed the sheriff had a preconceived idea about Maisy's attacker, and it was often a barrier he found hard to penetrate. "Let's go upstairs where it's more private," Beau suggested. "Maisy, Mrs. McGraw is still up there."

The two men walked upstairs in silence. Sheriff Garrett stood at the top of the stairs and took in his luxurious surroundings. "I've never been up here before," he said quietly. "It's…a lot," he said, and Beau knew he was referring to the opulent surroundings.

"I want to show you something," Beau told the sheriff. "Doss was going through this ledger when we found him. Mrs. McGraw is in danger from this man. He kidnapped her and held her hostage for days." He pointed to the dark bruise on Maisy's face. "He did that a short time ago, trying to get away."

The sheriff stared at Maisy's injury. "I'll get the doc here—he can write up a report for me." He then moved to the other side of the desk. He leaned in and read the parts of the ledger that were visible.

"I haven't touched a thing," Beau said. "For your information, I have been secured to protect Mrs. McGraw. You also need to see the will her late husband left."

Tommy Garrett stared at him, curiosity all over his face. "Sounds like this could be complicated. You'd better tell me everything," he said, looking for more ledgers that might be available.

"There's a separate meeting room where you can talk," Maisy said, and pointed to a door off to the side. "I'll stay here if you don't mind." She closed her eyes and rested her head on the back of the chair.

The two men left her alone, but still close enough if there was a disturbance, they would know. Beau wasn't surprised at the level of luxury in the room. He assumed it was used to entertain the bank's more wealthy clients. He motioned for the sheriff to sit down.

Beau told the sheriff everything he knew, including the details of the will.

"Why would Callum do such a thing?" Sheriff Garrett demanded. "The man wasn't a fool."

Beau shrugged. "With no heir to leave the bank to, perhaps he felt he had no other choice. He certainly could have done better by his wife."

The sheriff pushed his hat back on his head. "I can't fathom it. I knew him well enough to know Callum

McGraw wouldn't bow to pressure. Not from Doss, nor anyone."

"What exactly happened to Callum McGraw?" Beau asked. "According to Maisy, it was sudden and unexpected."

"It certainly was. Doc Murphy did an autopsy, but couldn't find a cause of death. It was the strangest thing," Sheriff Garrett said, scratching his head. "Callum wasn't old. Early thirties."

"Could Doss have killed him?" Beau suspected foul play. Right now though, it seemed there was no proof.

"A week ago, I would have been adamant he wouldn't. After what you've told me, and what he's done recently, it's anyone's guess." The sheriff shook his head. "What's your plan now? You can't protect Mrs. McGraw alone. Not twenty-four hours a day. It's impossible."

"I have a team," Beau said. "We will keep her safe. My plan is to catch Doss as well, but Maisy is my priority." He stood, triggering an end to their discussion. "It's a sad fact he could be miles from here by now."

Beau reached out and shook the sheriff's hand. "Thank you for your time. I will keep you apprised of any changes. Hopefully Doss keeps away and makes things easier for Maisy."

Sheriff Garrett stood. "Thank you, Hardner. I look forward to hearing from you." He then went down the stairs, and left the building.

Beau knew what he needed to do next, but wasn't prepared to leave Maisy unprotected. He hurried down the stairs to the area customers came to carry out their transactions. "You," he said, pointing to the young man who'd helped earlier. "I need your help. What is your name?"

"Charlie, Sir. Charlie Hogan. Is Mrs. McGraw alright?" The young man seemed genuinely concerned.

"Charlie," Beau said. "She has a massive bruise on her face, but apart from that she's fine. I need you to run an errand for me." He scribbled out a note and gave Charlie the address where he was to deliver it. It wasn't far, and the young man could walk there. "Go straight to this address, and don't stop anywhere along the way. When you get back, I'll update you and the other staff on what is happening."

"Yes, Sir," Charlie said, then turned away.

"And Charlie," Beau said firmly. "Stop calling me sir. My name is Beau."

"Yes, Sir, Beau," Charlie said as he left the building.

Beau sighed. At least things were moving along, but there was far too much to be done to keep Maisy safe.

Chapter Five

Maisy sat on the comfortable chair in her husband's office. She was still dazed from what happened, although what that was, she wasn't certain.

There was a large bruise on one side of her face according to Beau. Caused by Otis Doss. Maisy shook her head in astonishment. Since marrying Callum, her life had changed immensely. Since his death, it had been for the worse.

Now, with Otis trying to get her to sign over the bank to him, she didn't know what to think. Beau Hardner had come along at the right time, even if she had been suspicious of him in the beginning. As it turned out, the man was a godsend. What she would have done without him, Maisy really didn't know.

One thing she was certain of, and that was Otis had to be kept away from the bank, its ledgers, and its money.

Maisy gasped. Beau stood at the top of the stairs, along with Doc Murphy. He stared at her. "We didn't mean to startle you," he said as the pair stepped toward her.

"It's not that," she told him. "I have remembered something." She rubbed a hand across her forehead trying to dispel the headache that was forming. "Otis has keys to the bank. That gives him access to the vault and the safe with all the ledgers. He stepped into the role of bank manager immediately after Callum died."

"That was convenient," Beau muttered. "Don't worry about the keys. I'll get the locksmith here today. The more I learn about Otis Doss, the more I despise the man."

Doc Murphy stepped forward, interrupting the conversation. "Let me look at this injury," he said as he squatted in front of her. He gently touched the side of Maisy's face. She couldn't help but flinch. "I'm sorry, Mrs. McGraw. I just needed to check how bad it was." He then reached into his medical bag and handed her a small brown bottle. "Add this lavender oil to the bruise a few times a day. It will bring the bruise out quickly, and take much of the pain away."

"Thank you, Doctor," Maisy said, as she rubbed a hand across her forehead again.

He watched her every move. "Do you have a headache?" It was as though he could read her mind.

"It's not too bad," Maisy said, brushing his concerns aside.

He turned to Beau. "Did you see what happened?"

Beau stiffened. "Doss shoved Maisy aside, and she landed on the hard wood at the top of the stairs. If she'd been even slightly closer to the stairs, she would have fallen down them."

"Did she hit her head?" Doc Murphy demanded.

"It's a possibility," Beau said. "She certainly landed close to the edge."

Doc Murphy felt around her head. "There's a lump here," he said gruffly. "How many fingers am I holding up?" the doctor asked Maisy.

Her eyes weren't focusing well, but she could see it was two. "Two fingers. No, three," she said, then leaned back on the comfortable chair. All she wanted was to go home and get some sleep.

"I'm holding up one finger, Mrs. McGraw. You have a concussion," Doc Murphy said. "You need to sleep it off for at least three days. In a dark room."

Maisy sighed, then began to stand. It was then the dizziness overtook her. Before she knew what was happening, she was being held, and then lifted. "I've got you," Beau said, then Maisy felt herself being carried, and eventually laid down.

"Where am I?" she asked, confusion setting in.

"In your husband's meeting room. You can lay on the sofa until I can get you home," he told her. "I have arrangements to make for your safety before that can happen."

After setting her down, Maisy heard the curtains being pulled closed. She tried to keep her eyes open, but it was difficult. She was soon asleep and oblivious to whatever else was going on.

When she awoke, Maisy glanced about. The room was dark—the curtains were closed, and so was the door. She didn't recall anything after Doc Murphy examined her at the bank. Now she was confused. Exactly where was she? It was too dark to make anything out.

She pulled herself to a sitting position on the side of the bed, but dizziness overtook her. She remembered the last time she felt like this. It was in her husband's office. After that, there was a huge blank. Maisy laid down again, but in her efforts to do so, knocked into the side cupboard. The loud bang that followed reverberated through her head.

It was then the door flew open and a man stood in the doorway.

At first she believed it to be Otis Doss, only he was a runt of a man. This person was big and solid. With her head aching, she tried to focus, but it was impossible. "Are you alright?" the man asked. The voice was familiar, but Maisy couldn't recall why.

"Who…who's there?" she asked, trepidation clear in her voice.

"Maisy," he said. "It's me—Beau Hardner." He stepped further into the room.

With her mind swirling the way it was, Maisy couldn't think straight. "Beau Hardner?" she repeated. Trying to remember was making her head hurt even more.

He came closer and sat on the side of the bed. "My team and I are here to protect you from Otis Doss."

Now she remembered. "Of course," she said, her words seeming to slur a little. "What time is it?"

"It's late. I'll get you something to eat and drink. Doc Murphy says you have to stay in a dark room for a few days."

Beau's voice was soothing, unlike Otis whose voice grated on her. "Thank you," Maisy told him. "I appreciate it."

Maisy closed her eyes, and drifted off to sleep again.

Chapter Six

It had been one heck of a day.

Beau had gone from strolling around town to rescuing a lady in distress. While she'd slept, he pulled his team together and instructed them, had all the bank locks changed, as well as the house—in case Doss had keys to there as well—and updated the bank staff to the situation.

His four trusted security staff were already in place, and Beau was confident they would carry out their duties well. Those men had been with him for a long time, and knew what he expected of them.

He strolled into the kitchen to find something for Maisy to eat. He'd lit the cook stove when they'd arrived, so the kettle was boiling already. Rifling through the cupboards didn't turn up a lot of options. Maisy had been forced to stay in her hotel room recently, so it made sense.

"There's not much in the way of food," Bear, one of his team, said. "I checked earlier. There's some tinned food in there, but not a lot."

"Well," Beau said firmly, "that will have to be remedied. We'll be here for at least a few days, likely more. Catching that mongrel is our goal, but protecting Mrs. McGraw is our priority."

Beau reached into his jacket pocket and pulled out a wad of cash. "Take this and go to the mercantile. I trust you to get whatever we need." He handed Bear a decent amount of money, then made tea for Maisy.

He heard the front door close behind his trusted worker, and then the click of the lock. The problem with large houses like this one, was ensuring an *unwanted visitor* wasn't somewhere in the house already. Cole, another of his men, stood guard at the back entrance, but Beau knew Doss could be literally anywhere in this building.

He poured the tea the way Maisy liked it and found a cookie to serve with it. She needed to eat, even if it was only a small amount for now.

Pushing the bedroom door open with his foot, he entered the darkened room. It was then a thought struck him. With the possibility of Maisy's attacker striking again, how quickly could he, or any of his men, get to her before Otis Doss did any damage? Or even murdered Maisy?

The thought had his heart racing. He hurried into the room and placed the hot beverage on the side table. Maisy murmured in her sleep, then rolled toward him. As she looked up, she screamed.

"It's fine, Maisy," Beau said gently. "It's only me. Beau. I've brought you some tea, and something to eat. I've sent one of my men to get some real food—there's nothing much here."

He heard her sigh, then Maisy tried to sit up. Beau put a hand behind her, trying to make it easier for her.

It was then Cole rushed into the room. Beau saw the gun in his hand, and shuddered. What if that had been Doss? It confirmed two things for him. First, it took too long for his men to get from their post to the bedroom. And two, someone needed to be in the room at all times.

That someone would be Beau.

Oh, he knew Maisy would object. Having an unmarried man in the bedroom of a married woman, or even an unmarried one, went against all the rules of propriety. Surely there could be an exception to the rule in such dire circumstances?

Even having his men in the house without her husband would have tongues wagging. There was little he could do about it, since her husband was dead. It was then an idea came to him, but first he needed to seek legal advice on her behalf.

He would settle his client with her tea, and when she felt more comfortable, he would breach the subject.

Beau was certain he already knew her answer, but felt compelled to try.

~*~

"What? No!" Maisy almost screeched when Beau breached the subject. He'd brought Callum's lawyer, with him, to go over the conditions of her husband's will. Jonas Adamson was at first appalled when Beau explained his plan, but agreed it would stop Otis Doss in his tracks.

"As it stands now," Jonas said carefully, "if anything happens to you, the bank automatically goes to Otis. It's all there in your husband's will." He waved the will in front of her as if to ensure Maisy knew what he was talking about. "If you go along with Mr. Hardner's suggestion, Otis no longer has a reason to dispose of you." He leaned back in his chair and sighed. Beau knew this would be a difficult discussion, especially with Maisy still unwell. The lawyer assured him it was legal to do so with her in such a condition.

Maisy leaned against the pillows that supported her head and sighed. "How would it work? Of course I want to rid myself of the burden of my husband's will, but this seems rather extreme." Beau heard the defeat in her voice, and frankly, he didn't blame her.

Jonas leaned forward. "Should you remarry, your new husband is automatically the beneficiary of the bank. You will no longer have ownership, meaning Otis no longer has a reason to want to harm you."

Beau watched Maisy's every move. She didn't seem impressed with the entire situation. "I hadn't planned to remarry so soon after my husband's death." Her eyes shone with unshed tears, and Beau knew if it wasn't for the slight opening of the bedroom door, he wouldn't even see them.

Jonas glanced at Beau. "As I understand it, this will be a marriage of convenience." He turned to Beau who nodded. "That being the case, after the danger is over, you can have the marriage annulled. That is provided you don't…er, consummate the marriage."

Maisy gasped, and Beau's heart hammered in his chest. Even from the moment he'd thought of the idea, he knew she would be unhappy. No matter what, he had to protect her, and this was the best way he could think of, without ruining her reputation.

"What of my possessions, my home, and everything else I own?" Maisy asked, her voice low. "Do they also become the property of my husband?" She faced Jonas, but her eyes were on Beau.

"I'm afraid they do," Jonas said. "We could add a caveat to the will to the contrary, but then you'll be in the same situation all over again."

"I'm willing to sign an agreement," Beau said, but Jonas waved him aside.

"Then you might as well leave things as they are."

Beau knew he was right. They needed to marry and void the current will immediately. They also needed to ensure Otis Doss was held accountable for his actions.

Maisy swallowed so loud everyone in the room must have heard it. "Go ahead and make arrangements. I can't take much more of this," she said quietly.

Jonas stood. "I'll get all the documentation ready. Let me know when the wedding will be held."

"As soon as Maisy is up to it," Beau said firmly. "The sooner the better. We need to stop Otis Doss in his tracks."

He'd avoided marriage all his life, and felt pushed into a corner, despite it being his idea. Beau reminded himself it would only be temporary—until Doss was caught and locked away. Then they would get an annulment and get on with their separate lives.

Strangely, his heart felt hollow at the mere thought of never seeing Maisy McGraw again. That bothered him immensely.

Chapter Seven

Now fully recovered, Maisy stood next to Beau at the front of the small church in Pleasant Valley. Her heart broke for what she had to do to save herself. She was convinced Callum would be happy she'd taken this step to protect herself, and the bank.

He would be appalled at the actions of Otis Doss. According to what Callum told her after they'd married, Otis had been a godsend. He'd ensured the daily running of the bank, and completed the ledgers at the end of each day.

It made Maisy wonder if she should have an accountant go over those same ledgers.

"Ahem, Maisy?" Preacher Harry Dougherty cleared his throat, and Maisy glanced at him. "Just say *I do*," he whispered. "That is, if you agree," he quickly added.

She turned to face Beau Hardner. He seemed as unhappy about this marriage as she was, and yet they both agreed it was necessary.

"I do. Of course, I do," she said hastily.

"I do, too," Beau said, not waiting for his cue.

"Well then," Preacher Dougherty said. "You may kiss your bride."

Beau glanced at Maisy, his expression one of regret, then leaned in and brushed his lips over hers. As kisses went, that one was quite lame, but understandably so, given their circumstances. And their reason for marrying. Although the preacher had no idea of the scheme they'd put in place. The details would be kept between the newlyweds, the lawyer, and Beau's own security staff. Most likely Beau would also tell the sheriff.

What most people would know is they were married. Nothing more. To be honest, she'd feel better if everyone did know. That way, they were less likely to judge her for remarrying so soon after her husband had died in mysterious circumstances. Would the townsfolk now turn around and blame her for his death?

Maisy certainly hoped not. She wasn't even around when it happened. She was at home, and Callum was at the bank. According to Otis, he'd moments earlier finished a mug of coffee. Doctor Murphy declared it must have been a heart attack—there were no signs of foul play, nor did he have any injuries.

It was quite perplexing. Not to mention distressing.

Beau hooked his arm through hers, and they walked out of the church. Apart from two of his men, who acted as witnesses, no one was there to see them marry. It was probably for the best.

The moment they were outside, Maisy breathed in the fresh air. Inside, she'd felt stifled, and she knew why. She felt almost as though she was forced into this marriage, although she could have said no at any time. No one had forced her, not even Beau. It was totally her decision, but Maisy couldn't see any other way out of her situation. She only hoped Otis discovered she'd married, and left her alone.

She hadn't asked for any of this, and had no idea why Callum had changed his will to include Otis. She shook her head at the thought.

Beau squeezed her hand. "Are you alright?"

She turned and faced him. "Just thinking about Otis and what he did to me." She shook her head again. "Could Otis have forced Callum to change his will?"

"You knew him, I didn't. Do you think that's possible?" Beau studied her then, and it made Maisy squirm.

"He wasn't the sort to give in to heavy tactics, so I doubt it. Unless…" The mere thought hit her in the heart. "What if Otis threatened to harm me?" Maisy held back a sob.

Beau pulled her close and Maisy immediately felt comforted. "I suppose that's possible, but surely he would have gone to the sheriff afterwards and reported it." Beau rubbed a hand across his stubbled chin. "I need to look into this further. For now, we need to celebrate our marriage."

Maisy stared at him. "Celebrate? I thought we were going to keep it quiet." At least, that's what she hoped. Except not telling anyone meant Otis wouldn't find out he was no longer in line to inherit the bank. And wasn't that what this whole ordeal was about? Marrying her had automatically removed Otis from any chance of getting his grubby hands on the bank Callum had built up from scratch.

Jonas Adamson, her lawyer, was already working on a new will, and ensuring Otis Doss would never inherit a thing. Maisy's concern now was that her husband had put himself in the line of fire. However, with Otis completely wiped from receiving any part of Callum's estate, there would be no point him even trying.

"Come on," Beau said, his arm tightening around her. "We'll have a bite to eat, then head straight to the lawyer's office. The more difficult we make it for Otis to get his hands on you and your property, the happier I will be."

Despite having three men protecting her, Maisy felt exposed simply crossing the street from the church to the diner. She glanced around ensuring no one was there, trying to harm her. By no one, she specifically meant Otis. She would put nothing past him.

As they reached the door to the diner, she breathed a sigh of relief. It was then a bullet flew past her cheek. Without warning, Beau pulled her inside as he swore under his breath. Cole and Bear took off to find the shooter. Knowing Otis, Maisy was certain they wouldn't find him. He seemed to have a way of slipping through their fingers.

"Get down under the table," Beau shouted. Maisy didn't protest. She had hoped their marriage would be the end of her troubles. She now understood why Beau insisted they be seen in public celebrating their marriage.

"Is this what my life is going to be like from now on?" Maisy asked as she cowered under the table.

"Not if I can help it," he said, then pulled a gun from its holster. Beau stood at the window and glanced about. "There he is, the weasel." He pointed to the roof of a store, which stood opposite. She stared in horror as her new husband went to the door and pointed his gun in that direction.

"When will it all end?" she whispered to herself, more afraid than ever. Even when he had tried to force her to sign over the bank, Otis had not once produced a firearm. Although he'd hinted at having one in his jacket. Maisy couldn't be sure it was the truth.

Beau came back inside and glanced at her under the table. "Now we wait and see if Bear and Cole catch the coward," he said gruffly. "I should have known he'd do something like this. Especially if he realized we'd married. His opportunity to control the bank is long gone. Now we need to catch him and march the filthy polecat to the sheriff's office."

Maisy knew Beau was right. "He's more dangerous now, isn't he?" she asked quietly. "The moment I step out onto the boardwalk, he'll shoot me down. Before the paperwork is all in place."

Beau scratched his head. "You could be right. I have a solution for that." As Bear crossed the road toward the diner, Maisy wondered what Beau's solution could be.

Bear entered, and Beau immediately went to him. The other man retreated outside and soon disappeared. It wasn't long before he returned. He ushered her lawyer ahead of him. Jonas entered the diner carrying his briefcase.

Were they going to tend to her legal documentation here in the diner? Whatever kept Otis away from her worked for Maisy.

Beau led Maisy to a table away from the window and prying eyes. He ordered refreshments for everyone, then Jonas got to work.

Chapter Eight

"Thank you, Jonas," Beau said as he stood. "My men will escort you back to your office, and ensure you are safe." Jonas offered his hand, and Beau shook it. "All we need to do now is catch Otis Doss and hand him over to the sheriff."

"That," Jonas said, "would be a relief. He obviously doesn't know he would get nothing under the terms of the previous will—should he have been found guilty of murder."

Beau stared at him. "He's too smart for that. At least I thought he was, but now he's desperate. We both know desperate men are capable of anything."

The door to the diner opened, and Sheriff Tommy Garrett entered. "I can't find any sign of him. No idea where the fool would have fled to." He shook his head then. "I'm still having trouble connecting Otis Doss with this behavior. He has never been in trouble with the law."

"Are you certain about that?" Beau asked, wondering if that were even true. "Has he always lived here?"

"No. No, he hasn't," the sheriff said. "He arrived here around the same time I did." He closed his eyes momentarily. "It would be a couple of years ago now, maybe longer. Otis has been a model citizen up until now. I will do some digging. This is all very hard to swallow." He was gone as quickly as he'd arrived.

Beau stared after him, then he gazed along the roofline of the buildings opposite. He saw nothing. Bear left the diner and hurried across the road. Cole was on his heels. "We'll wait for them to return," he told Maisy. Better safe than sorry—that was his motto and always would be.

So help him, if Otis Doss turned up, it would take all his effort not to strangle the poor excuse of a man. "Have you had enough to eat? We can stay a little longer if you want."

Except he could see by the expression on her face, Maisy was ready to go home. She'd told him she felt safe there, although with the way her attacker had behaved lately, Beau couldn't be certain she was safe anywhere right now.

"I'm ready to leave," she whispered. Maisy was a shell of the woman he'd met days ago. The constant stress of the situation was getting to her, and Beau could understand that.

The other two men entered the diner moments later. "All clear," Cole said.

Beau heard Maisy sigh with relief. "Ready?" he asked.

"As I'll ever be," she said, then with her arm clasped tightly through his, they left the diner as a group. His men would be ever vigilant. If Maisy's attacker turned up, they would know about it, and eliminate the threat. Those were the instructions he'd given them, but Beau didn't dare relay that information to Maisy. He wasn't sure she would agree with his tactics. From his point of view, it would be the best thing to ensure her safety.

~*~

"It is so good to be back home," Maisy said once they were all inside the house.

Bear and Cole went through every room to ensure they had no unwanted visitors. They might have changed all the locks, but the house was still vulnerable via the windows. All Doss had to do was smash a window and he would be inside.

What Beau really needed was more men. Except his other two men, Hawk and Trapper, were guarding the bank. He knew Maisy would never forgive herself if Doss got in and attacked her staff, or even the customers.

There were three of them here, and that should be enough, except that slimy polecat seemed to find Maisy wherever she happened to be. "Put your copy of the paperwork in the safe," Beau instructed. "We don't want it hanging around for Doss to find."

She turned to him with a look of pure terror on her face. "He…he can't get in, can he?"

He stepped toward her, his arms opened wide. "No, of course not. I don't know why I even suggested it." His new wife settled herself in his arms, and rested her head on his chest. As much as Beau knew he shouldn't be doing this, they were legally married, and if it made her feel better, then what was the problem?

"Thank you," she whispered as his heart thundered in his chest. "I needed that."

Truth be told, he did, too. Beau had protected many clients over the years, including high-profile women, and not once had he felt anything toward them. And yet, he had feelings for Maisy. Was it because of the situation she'd been placed in? He wasn't convinced. Although a unique situation, other women had been in fear of their lives, and he hadn't felt this way. Nor had he offered them the comfort of his arms.

Instead of letting her go, his arms tightened around her. Without his permission, his head went down, and he kissed her forehead. The moment his lips touched Maisy's skin, Beau knew he'd made the biggest mistake of his life.

~*~

Maisy pottered about in the kitchen. She seemed happy enough, and he was right there to ensure she was safe.

The moment the kettle boiled, she'd made each of the men coffee, and placed a plate of store-bought cookies in the middle of the table. "Thank you, Maisy. That is so kind of you," Beau said.

Bear and Cole muttered their thanks as well.

"What happens next?" Maisy asked as she sat with them and sipped her tea. "I can't stay locked up in my home forever."

"We wait," Beau said firmly. "I know it's difficult, but Doss will make a mistake, and that's when we'll find him." He reached across the table and covered her hand with his. The movement was not lost on his men. Their eyes followed his every movement.

Beau quickly pulled his hand back. He was acting like a man in love. Just because he'd married Maisy, didn't mean he could use it to his advantage. There was only one reason they'd married, and that was for propriety's sake. Her reputation had to be protected as much as Maisy herself.

"Have a cookie," she suddenly said into the silence. The atmosphere had suddenly become charged when he'd pulled his hand back. Truth be known, he'd made matters worse by doing so. "What shall we have for supper? I noticed some beef in the icebox. Anyone up for stew?"

"It's why I bought the beef, Mrs. McGr… er, Mrs. Hardner," Bear said, then slapped his mouth closed.

Maisy frowned. Did that mean she wasn't happy with being called by her new married name?

It was a tricky situation, and Beau understood that. They hadn't discussed what they should call Maisy. For the purposes of having people believe they were truly husband and wife, she needed to be known by his surname.

"Why don't you call me Maisy," she said, her gaze taking in everyone at the table. She was clearly uncomfortable being addressed as Mrs. Hardner, and Beau could understand her reasoning. Maisy hadn't been a widow all that long. Heck. She'd only been married six months when her husband died under suspicious circumstances.

Suddenly, in the eyes of the townsfolk, she remarried. Beau hoped and prayed they didn't believe she had anything to do with her husband's death. It was apparent now, everything that happened was down to Otis Doss. Somehow, he'd weaseled his way into Callum McGraw's circle of trust, and then murdered him. Apart from protecting Maisy, he had to find a way to prove Callum died at the hands of his former assistant. He was convinced that was the case.

"Where can I find paper and pen?" Beau suddenly asked. He needed more manpower, and needed them quickly.

Maisy tilted her head to the side. "I'll get it for you," she said as she attempted to stand.

He reached for her hand again, halting her departure. "No hurry. Finish your tea first." He felt the eyes of his men again, but this time Beau didn't remove his hand.

Chapter Nine

Maisy's heart raced. It shouldn't be this way, she knew, but whenever Beau was near, she felt …different. Happier.

She glanced at his hand covering hers, and a shiver went down her spine. Her husband was only months in the ground and already she had feelings for another man? *You married him, didn't you?* a voice in her head asked. But Maisy knew the two did not necessarily go hand in hand.

Beau had insisted they marry for both propriety and her safety. It was totally different from marrying for love. When all of this was over, when Otis was caught and jailed, their marriage would be annulled. It would be like it never happened.

As the last sip of tea slid down her throat, Maisy stood. She would get the supplies Beau needed, and then start on supper. It had been some time since she'd spent time in a kitchen—Callum had insisted on employing a cook. It was more for appearances than anything. Maisy had little to fill her days, and cooking would have helped.

They had a cook and a housekeeper, which left little for her to do. Boredom soon took over, and Maisy suggested she help at the women's auxiliary. Except that didn't sit well with her husband. She would be working below her calling.

Why they hadn't discussed all these things before their marriage, she didn't know. Maisy truly wished she had. It hadn't taken long for her to regret having married the bank manager, who was never affectionate toward her. All he was interested in was appearances, and it seemed Maisy was part of that plan.

Rummaging through Callum's desk drawer, Maisy found a notepad and handed it over to Beau who was right behind her. She indicated the pen and ink that sat on the large mahogany desk. "Help yourself," she said quietly, then left him alone in the room.

She went straight back to the kitchen and began to wash up. Soon she would start supper. Rummaging through the cupboards was new for Maisy. She had never cooked in this kitchen—Cook chased her away when she tried. Today though, she needed to locate the pot she needed, along with sharp knives and chopping boards. It couldn't be that hard.

The moment she had everything she needed, Maisy went to the pantry. She hoped Bear had bought everything she needed. She spun around at the sound of someone behind her.

"Sorry, Maisy," Bear said, regret in his voice. "Just checking if you need anything else from the mercantile. Beau sent me to ask."

Her heart pounded, but soon calmed. Beau assured her no one could get into the house, including Otis Doss. She had three men guarding her, each of them extremely experienced at protecting their clients. "Let me check," Maisy said, trying to ignore the fact she had been terrified only moments ago.

She leaned down and plucked the vegetables required, then pulled the meat from the icebox and loaded up Bear's arms with everything. Next she checked the flour. "Urgh!" She grimaced at what she saw. "That's disgusting," Maisy declared.

Bear leaned in to see what had horrified her. "Weevils. I can get fresh flour," he said. "It won't take long."

Maisy nodded. "There's plenty to do before I need the flour anyway," she said.

"I'll let Beau know," he said, then headed toward the kitchen.

Weevils were the bane of any kitchen. Maisy knew she would have to check the other supplies now, to ensure the evil creatures had not infiltrated other food sources. Right now though, she had a meal to prepare.

Placing the pot on the stove to heat up, Maisy stoked the stove to ensure good heat. She would normally use bacon fat to cook the meat, but today all she had available was butter. It would only take a spoonful. She set about cutting the meat into cubes, then threw them into the pan.

After braising the meat, Maisy set about preparing the vegetables. She added them to the pot, along with some water. Then she sat down for a brief reprieve. It had been a long time since she'd been allowed to cook, but doing so brought her great satisfaction.

"Bear is going to the mercantile for flour and also sending a telegraph for me. Is there anything else you need?" Beau asked as he stood in the doorway.

She glanced up at him and smiled. Maisy couldn't deny her fake husband was a good looking man. He was tall and broad. He didn't smile much, but when he did, her heart tumbled and warmth filled her.

Maisy scrambled to her feet. She couldn't sit around woolgathering like this. "Let me check the pantry for apples. I want to make a pie for dessert." She hurried into the pantry and away from the influences of Beau's presence. She also checked the icebox again while she was there. "I need four large cooking apples, milk, and cream," she said, then sat back down at the table.

Beau walked toward her and sat down. "Is everything alright?" he asked gently. "You don't seem yourself."

Maisy raised her eyebrows. Despite their recent marriage, he didn't know her at all. The pair had known each other for such a short period of time, it would be laughable if it hadn't been so serious. "The situation, I guess. And shock. Who would have thought Otis Doss would turn on me like this?" Closing her eyes, Maisy tried to shake away the memories of what she'd endured at the hands of that man.

If Callum had still been alive, none of this would have happened. He would have protected her. Maisy sighed. She wondered if that was true. Callum, she had now realized, was self-centered. Callum was interested in Callum, and what others could do for him. Being rich seemed to make him believe he was far better than everyone else, and deserved whatever came his way.

It was a hard truth to swallow, but Beau Hardner had done far more for her in a short time, than Callum ever had. And that was even before she'd employed him to protect her. It made Maisy stop and think about her relationship with her first husband. Did he even love her? Or was she merely someone for him to show off and boast about?

The thought made her wonder if her marriage to Callum was as fake as her marriage to the man sitting next to her now. "I think I need to rest," she said, not ready to disclose the revelation. "I need to stir the stew first." Maisy went to the stove and stirred the food, adding more water as she did so.

She was alone far too much—that was the problem. Being alone meant giving in to her thoughts. It wasn't something she wanted to do, especially given her present circumstances.

Maisy heard Beau shuffle up behind her. "Mmmmm, smells good," he said, then put his arms around her. Was he taking liberties because of the situation, or was he merely trying to console her? She chose to believe the latter.

Turning around in his arms, Maisy leaned into him. No matter his motivation, he made her feel safe. And comforted. More than anything, both were important to her at the moment. "What's going on?" Beau asked gently, his arms tightening around her.

Shaking her head, Maisy didn't want to tell him, but Beau seemed to have a way of getting information from her. "Callum didn't love me," she said on a sob.

Beau lifted her chin and wiped her tears away. "I doubt that," he began, but she interrupted him.

"I've thought about it. He never held me the way you do, and the only time he kissed me was at our wedding."

Beau's eyes opened wide in astonishment. "The man was a fool," he said, and held her the way a husband should. A real husband—one who loved his wife. Not a fake husband who was only pretending to love her for all eternity.

Chapter Ten

Beau's heart pounded. Holding Maisy like this did things to him. He needed to stop doing it, but it comforted her. If he was truthful with himself, it made him feel good, too.

He thought about what she'd said—that her husband had not shown any affection toward her. The words he spoke were true—anyone who shunned Maisy was a fool. An absolute idiot. By all accounts she was beautiful, inside and out.

Except for those dreadful widow gowns she wore.

"Maisy," he said as he glanced down into her face. She lifted her gaze to meet his. "Now that we're married, you need to stop wearing black." What she would think, he wasn't sure.

"It's a fake marriage," she whispered, as though afraid someone might hear her.

"To the rest of the town, it is very real. You looked beautiful in the gown you wore for our marriage ceremony. You must surely have more like that?"

"You're right," Maisy said firmly, her voice devoid of all emotion, then looked down at herself. She'd changed out of the pretty gown, and back into black the moment they returned home. "I hadn't really thought about it. I guess it's become automatic." She pulled out of his arms and headed toward the bedroom, telling Bear her additional supply needs along the way.

As much as he knew he shouldn't, Beau missed holding her. He followed Maisy to her dressing room, then stood back to stare at her selection of clothes. "You have more clothes than I've seen in my life," he said, but not in an accusing tone. One entire section held all her mourning clothes, and he was distracted by those. "You should get rid of those," he said, pointing to them, and Maisy stared at him.

"Won't I need them after our marriage is annulled?"

She appeared genuinely confused. If Beau had his way, they wouldn't have their marriage annulled, but this was a business agreement of sorts. He'd told her that's what they would do, and he had to stick to the plan. "Not unless you plan to kill me off," he said with a chuckle.

"I can donate them to the church," she said tight-lipped. "I'm sure someone will get use from them."

Beau watched as Maisy searched for a different colored gown to wear. It was clear she couldn't make a decision. Was she always like that, or had recent circumstances caused her confusion? He guessed the choice between black or black was an easy one. "May I?" he asked, then reached for a sky blue gown. "This one goes perfectly with your eyes."

He stared into her face, his eyes not moving from hers. It wasn't the truth, and he knew it. Blue didn't particularly go with hazel eyes, but he wanted to get her out of anything drab. It made her look years older, and surely pulled down her mood. He wondered if it had affected her in other ways.

"You need to leave," Maisy told him. "I can't change with you in here." She held the gown in her arms, ready to put it on, and studied him, as if daring him to protest.

"I'll be right outside the door," Beau told her. He left reluctantly, but with no other way in, Doss would not gain entry to Maisy's dressing room. Once outside the door, he shook his head in disbelief. The rich lived in a completely different way to everyone else. Beau knew he could never be happy living this way. It was too formal, and there was far too much at stake. The upkeep on the house alone would be tremendous. Still, if you had the sort of money to buy such a house, you'd likely have enough to maintain it.

It wasn't long before Maisy exited her dressing room. He stared at her as she stood there in the colorful gown. She was a different woman than the one who'd been wearing black since the day they'd met. "You look beautiful," he said, and meant it. She took his breath away. It was then Beau knew he had a difficult job ahead of him.

Keeping his hands off his wife would be one of the most challenging things he'd ever done.

~*~

They sat quietly in the sitting room, neither saying a word. Maisy read a book, and Beau simply sat beside her. Boredom was never an option, since he was there to protect her. Every now and then, Maisy jumped up from her seat and headed to the kitchen to stir the stew she had cooking for super.

Beau followed her each time.

This time she removed an apple pie from the oven, and added the bread to be cooked. They'd spent a lot of the afternoon in the kitchen, between the stew needing to be stirred, and Maisy preparing the bread for supper. After she mixed the dough initially, it had to be set aside to rise, she'd told him. Then she banged it out and set it aside again. Until today, Beau had no idea making a loaf of bread was so much work.

He now understood why families who were well off employed a cook. The wife was constantly dealing with meals. Beau hated to see his wife spending so much time cooking. Although, to be honest, Maisy seemed to enjoy it.

The moment the bread was in the oven, she began to set the table. As much as Beau preferred each of his men stayed at their post, they had to eat. If Doss did get in, which was highly unlikely, they would secure him quickly.

As much as Beau didn't want Maisy to be a decoy, he did wish her attacker would try and get to her. They would never catch him otherwise. He might be a runt of a man, but he did have brains. The fact he was able to fool Callum McGraw and secure the position of assistant bank manager told Beau a lot about the criminal.

It made him wonder if the sheriff managed to find out anything about Otis Doss's history. If Beau had to guess, he would say Doss had done something like this before. You don't suddenly become a murderer—it was usually something the criminal has worked his way up to. At least in Beau's experience.

"Supper is ready," Maisy said a few minutes later, as she removed the bread from the oven. She added butter to the table, and placed the still warm bread on a wooden tray and placed it in the middle of the table. "I'll get you to cut the bread, if you don't mind," she said.

Beau's mouth was watering just thinking about it. How long had it been since he'd had a home cooked meal? He couldn't even remember.

Beau was about to alert Cole to the meal when he stuck his head in the kitchen. "Smells delicious in here," he said.

"It certainly does," Beau said, and noticed Maisy smiling. It was one of the few times he'd seen her happy since the day they met. Not that she had a lot to smile about recently. "Can you call Bear? I'm sure he'll be hungry, too."

Cole left them alone, and Maisy began dishing up the stew. A large bowl for each of the men, and a smaller serving for herself. Now they were alone again, Beau felt the pangs of longing. He wanted nothing more than to hold Maisy. It was becoming difficult to keep his distance. But he would, he had to ensure he did.

What would happen tonight when they were in the same bedroom, he wasn't sure. With only the one bed, his restraint would be sorely tested.

"Everyone sit down," she said as Bear and Cole entered the kitchen. "The bigger bowls are for you men," she said, and they each found their place.

Once they were all seated, Maisy reached across and took Beau's hand on the one side, and Bear's on the other. At first Beau was startled, not understanding what was going on. Then he realized she was waiting to say the blessing, and reached for Cole's hand. Bear did the same.

After the blessing, everyone began to eat. Maisy watched them, a smile on her face. "Why do they call you Bear?" she asked.

Bear shrugged his shoulders. Cole and Beau laughed. "Because he is like a bear with a sore head first thing in the morning," Beau said.

"And he eats like a bear," Cole added.

They all laughed, except for Bear. "My mother always called me Bear," he said. "She told me I was big as a bear." He shrugged again and went back to his food. "This is good," he said as he continued to tuck in.

These were good men. They'd worked for Beau for some time now, and he hoped they'd be with him for a long time to come.

Not that he would tell Maisy, but all three were listening out for sounds of a break in. They might appear undisturbed about Otis Doss, but they were continually vigilant.

Chapter Eleven

The moment she'd reached for Beau's hand, Maisy knew she'd done the wrong thing. Sparks ran up her arm when she'd clasped her hand in Beau's. His look of astonishment alerted her that he too, had felt it.

Or was he simply startled about having her reach for him? Maisy decided it was the latter. There was no reason for her to think there was anything more to it. Their marriage was a complete sham, designed to keep Otis at arm's length. Although Maisy wasn't convinced it would be the case. Had she been told this would happen, she'd have laughed it off as a joke.

Only now, it was no laughing matter. In fact, it had quickly become a life and death situation. If she hadn't escaped her hotel room, and landed in the arms of Beau Hardner, Maisy knew where she would be now. Six feet underground.

A shudder ran through her, and Maisy's first instinct was to run. Only Beau held her tightly. It made her wonder if he'd felt the shock wave that had engulfed her momentarily.

"You alright?" he whispered.

Maisy closed her eyes for mere seconds, then opened them. She nodded her head slightly. "I…I guess I'm not," she said, knowing this man could almost read her mind. "I'll be fine. Would you like more stew?" she asked. Maisy was already standing by this time. Luckily, she'd made plenty—three hands went up. She couldn't help but grin.

It was nice to cook for men who appreciated the food, and the effort. Not that she had anything else to do with her time. Apart from reading, there was little left for her to do. Until recently, she hadn't been home for some time. At least while she stayed in the hotel, she could call into the bank now and then to see how things were going.

Did Otis get fed up with her checking in on him? Was that why he took her hostage? In her own hotel room, no less. No wonder she hadn't been reported missing. "It was my fault," she mumbled, incredulous at her entire situation.

"What's your fault?" Beau asked. "I'm sure it wasn't, whatever it is." He reached for her hand, and Maisy didn't refuse him.

"No one knew I was missing because I'd moved into the hotel, and spent most of my time there." She shook her head sadly. That Otis Doss could do such a thing still disturbed her. Why did some men believe they have the right to abduct women and do whatever they wished with them?

"It most certainly is not your fault," Beau said, emphasizing the fact. "Only a madman would do something like that."

"I suppose you're right." Maisy reached across the table and took Beau's bowl. Then she refilled it with stew. She did the same for the other two men. Then she strolled to the kitchen counter and began to cut up the apple pie. It was still warm, and the aroma was enticing. After dishing out plenty of pie for each man, she collected their soiled bowls. These were big men with big appetites. The type of man she'd happily feed every day. Maisy served the pie and added a bowl of clotted cream to the center of the table.

Beau grabbed her wrist as she moved away. "You've outdone yourself, Maisy," he said. "The stew was flavorful and filling. The pie smells amazing." He looked at her quizzically. "Where did you learn to cook like this?"

"My parents' restaurant," Maisy said matter-of-factly. "After my mother died, I took over the kitchen completely." She could almost see the men drooling at her revelation. "I cook wholesome meals, nothing fancy," she told them, then sat down to eat her dessert.

"Looks pretty fancy to me," Bear said right before he shoved the last of his apple pie into his mouth.

A short time later, Maisy heard the sound of glass smashing. "That sounds to have come from Callum's office," she said urgently.

Cole and Bear were on their feet and gone in moments. Beau stayed by her side.

For the first time in several days, Maisy was scared. If Otis breached the house, was he doing it to kill her? Beau's arms went up around her, but this time Maisy did not feel comforted. Instead, she was downright petrified.

~*~

The sound of bullets flying terrified Maisy, and she tucked her head close to Beau's chest. Her entire body was shaking, and she couldn't do anything to stop it. Maisy shoved her fist in her mouth to stop herself from screaming.

"It's alright," Beau said gently as he rubbed a hand across her back. "He isn't in the house, I can assure you of that." A tear slipped down her cheek, and Beau wiped it away. "I promised to protect you from that polecat, and that's exactly what I'm doing." He held Maisy tight in his arms until the moment Bear entered the kitchen.

"He's gone," Bear said. "I'm certain it was Doss. He threw a rock through the window, but didn't count on anyone hearing it."

Cole stepped into the room moments later. "He also didn't count on anyone shooting at him," he told them.

"Was he hit?" Beau wanted to know.

Bear and Cole exchanged glances. "I think I grazed him," Cole said. "But I can't be sure—he was too far away by that time."

Keeping his arm around Maisy, he barked out orders. "Get that window replaced immediately. Get the others from the bank—I want them here tonight. The moment the additional men arrive tomorrow morning, get them here."

Maisy's head was swimming, but it was obvious Beau knew what he was doing. He glanced down at her. "Everything is under control," he said, lifting her chin with his fingers. She had no choice but to look into his face. "I'm sleeping in your bedroom tonight. No arguments."

Her heart pounded. They were married, there was no doubt about that. The plan was a marriage in name only until they caught Otis Doss, then an annulment. Sleeping in the same bed as Beau Hardner was not on the agenda.

Maisy wasn't sure she could cope with that.

Chapter Twelve

Beau felt her shaking, but there was nothing he could do about it except hold Maisy tightly. He understood how frightened she must be, especially given Doss had already held her hostage and tried to force her to sign the bank over to him.

It was now crystal clear he was intent on killing Maisy. It was the only option left to him to get his hands on the bank. Only now, Callum McGraw's will was null and void. Maisy was no longer the owner of the Pleasant Valley Bank. Beau was.

Not that he intended to keep it. Or stay married to Maisy. It was all a temporary situation, and would be resolved the moment Doss was captured and behind bars. More likely than not, he would hang for his crimes.

Maisy shrugged out of his arms. Beau hated to admit it, but he felt bereft at her loss. He liked holding Maisy this way, even though he knew he shouldn't.

She stood at the sink, her back to him. Maisy seemed intent on cleaning up the kitchen. His focus was on keeping her safe. Beau had already learned when Maisy decided to do something she forged ahead, despite the obstacles that got in her way.

Instead of insisting she stop, he helped clear the table. He leaned over the table and began to pick up the dessert bowls. Maisy did the same thing. Their hands brushed, and he felt it all the way up his arm.

Maisy stared into his eyes. She had beautiful eyes. His gaze wandered downward to her lips. They were far more inviting than they should be. His fake wife was beautiful. She was far too enticing for Beau's liking. Their marriage had been planned with nothing more than Maisy's safety in mind.

Instead, somewhere along the line, his heart hadn't listened to the instructions. Never before had Beau felt this way about any woman. It was highly unlikely it would happen again. Beau knew he had to be strong. For Maisy's sake. Walking away from her at the end of this ordeal was the only way. His job was similar to that of a marshal or sheriff—it was far too dangerous to involve a wife. Or children for that matter.

"Would you mind getting the cream?" Maisy asked, her voice low.

It was enough to bring him out of his thoughts and back to the present. "Of course," Beau said. "It would be my pleasure." He shook himself mentally. What a stupid thing to say. Had he lost the facility to talk properly, to think, along with losing his heart to this woman? He needed to give himself a stern talk, and it needed to be sooner than later.

~*~

Maisy prepared for bed, just as she normally would. Only it wasn't a normal night—far from it. Beau's heart raced. He had to stay in the same room as Maisy. He would try not to sleep, but it would be difficult. Staying awake for much longer meant he wouldn't function the way he needed to function. Even if he fell asleep, Beau would be wide awake if needed.

When the additional men he'd sent for arrived, Beau would be able to spread his team around better. Everyone would get the rest they required, which meant Maisy would be better protected.

"I'm going to bed," Maisy said on a yawn. She had changed into her nightgown and wore a pretty robe. Both would have cost more than an average worker's weekly wage. Beau wondered if she realized how privileged she really was.

He stared at her hair. It flowed down her back. How he would love to stroke it, but Beau knew he couldn't. "I'm coming with you," he answered instead, keeping his feelings to himself.

Maisy turned to face him. "You were serious about sleeping with me? I thought you were joking," she said, clearly surprised at his words. Then her cheeks turned pink.

Beau lifted a hand to caress her cheek, then pulled it back. As sweet as she looked when she blushed, he needed to keep his distance. "I said I would protect you, and I meant it," he said firmly, then ushered Maisy into the bedroom.

She began to undo her robe, then glanced up at him. "Turn around," she said firmly. It took all his effort to hold back a chuckle. Beau wasn't certain she would appreciate it. "You can turn back now," she said quietly. He turned back to find she'd climbed into bed. She had the bedding pulled up to her chin, and this time Beau almost did laugh. What did Maisy think he was going to do? He was here to protect her. There would be no shenanigans tonight.

Or any other night, he reminded himself. This was strictly a business arrangement. Nothing more, nothing less.

He kicked off his shoes and climbed onto the bed coverings, lying next to Maisy. "Don't worry about me," Beau said. "I'll be right here. Doss would be a fool to try and get to you."

She stared at him as Beau laid down on the pillow. "It's been a long time since I shared my bed with anyone," she said softly.

"We're not exactly sharing the bed," he said firmly. I'll be here, on the lookout." Hopefully, he didn't fall asleep. He'd been awake for far too long, and it was beginning to show.

Maisy turned away from him, and laid her head against the pillow. "I'm scared," she whispered.

Beau wasn't in the least surprised. He was afraid for her. Luckily, he had a good team of men. Unfortunately, Doss was as slimy as a snake. He had slipped through their hands too many times. Trouble was, he knew this town inside out. Beau and his team did not. They needed to remedy that— sooner than later.

Without thinking, Beau's arms went up around Maisy as she lay facing away from him. She scuttled closer to him, and his gut churned. The last thing he should be doing is holding her like this. Once her ordeal was over, they would arrange for an annulment, and he would be out of her life forever.

The mere thought of it twisted Beau's heart and shattered it into tiny pieces. It told him a lot—he had to keep his distance, and ensure he did not get any more involved than he already was. In fact, he should take a step back. How easy that would be to do, Beau wasn't sure. What he did know was he couldn't afford to fall in love with Maisy McGraw.

It was then he remembered she was Maisy Hardner, his wife. For not the first time, Beau truly wished the fantasy could become reality.

His arms tightened around Maisy, and she relaxed in his arms. His gun sat close by under the pillow, should Otis Doss be stupid enough to breach the house.

Beau fought to stay awake, but his body had other ideas. The mesmerizing sound of Maisy sleeping was the last thing he recalled before he fell into a deep sleep himself.

~*~

The breaking of glass woke Beau abruptly. He reached for his gun and waited. No matter what, he would not leave Maisy's side. It would be Doss's intention to get her alone—he likely thought she was in the room by herself. He was in for a shock.

Until moment's ago, Maisy too, was sound asleep. Now she was wide awake, her eyes opened wide with fear. He indicated for her to keep quiet. Beau crept out of the bed and glanced out the window. It was dawn, and the sun was still rising.

It confirmed what Beau already knew—Doss wasn't stupid. He waited until he believed everyone would be asleep and not prepared for an attack. A rude awakening awaited him. The bedroom door flew open, but Beau was ready for him.

Except Otis Doss didn't stand before him. This man was the last person he expected to see.

Chapter Thirteen

"Put your hands up!" Beau bellowed as Maisy's heart pounded.

"Don't shoot! I…I'm not armed." Maisy heard the fear in the man's voice. She'd closed her eyes against the onslaught she believed was about to happen. If she was going to die, she didn't want to see it coming. Now she opened her eyes abruptly.

Maisy's breath left her. "Charlie!" she gasped. "What are you doing here? Are you working with Otis?" she demanded. Why meek and mild Charlie Hogan would be helping Otis Doss, she would never know.

"I'm sorry," he said, regret clear in his voice. "He is holding my family hostage." At that moment, Maisy felt Charlie's pain. There was so much Otis Doss had been hiding about himself, and had only begun to reveal. "I don't want to hurt anyone, especially you, Mrs. McGraw," he said, sadness in his voice. "The gun he gave me is outside."

His hands still in the air, Beau patted him down. "No firearm," Beau told Hawk, who was headed their way.

"I came to warn you, and…" Charlie shuffled his feet on the floor. "to get help. My wife and children are in danger, and I didn't know what else to do."

"Sit down over there," Beau demanded of Charlie, pointing at a chair in the sitting room. Then he whispered something to Bear. The other man nodded. It wasn't long until he had Cole on one side, and Bear on the other.

Maisy sprang out of bed and put on her robe. She hurried into the kitchen and made coffee for everyone, Charlie included. "I'll go and dress," she told Beau after she'd done so. It was then he stopped her.

"I'd rather you stayed here where I can keep an eye on you," he told her.

Maisy was convinced something was afoot, but wasn't sure what. Of course Beau wasn't telling her everything, and that only served to annoy her. "And I'd rather dress," she said gruffly, then stormed out of the kitchen. There was no window or door into her dressing room from outside, so she wasn't sure what Beau's problem was. Otis couldn't get to her, and that was clearly his concern. She hurried in and closed the door, and spent as little time as possible on choosing a gown. It wasn't as though she was going anywhere, so no need to fuss. On second thought, she remembered Beau liked to see her in pretty colors.

The day had already begun badly, so she chose a pretty pastel color, hoping that would brighten her outlook. After dressing, she brushed her hair and fashioned it, placing a pretty clip at the back of her head. Lastly, she slipped into a pair of matching shoes.

She was already beginning to feel better.

When she opened the door to her dressing room, Maisy discovered Beau standing guard. He leaned in and whispered in her ear. "You look beautiful," he said, "but you're incredibly frustrating at times." Maisy couldn't help but smile, then continued on to the kitchen.

Beau followed her, trailing behind like a lost puppy. "Maisy," he finally said, "come and meet two more of my men. They arrived last night. Flynn and Wesley," he said, indicating each man. "This is Maisy."

"Nice to meet you," she told the two men, then turned to Beau. "I'm making breakfast. You can come as long as you're quiet," she told him firmly. Maisy heard the chuckles of her two new protectors. The moment they were in the kitchen, she turned on Beau. "Don't you think this is overkill. You now have four men here to protect me?"

"Six," he said, a sheepish look on his face. "The others will be along soon. Otis Doss is far too cunning. He has a lot at stake, but so do you." He ran a hand through his already mussed up hair. "For him, it's all about the money. In your case, it's your life." He stepped forward then, and Maisy knew he was going to hold her. "I don't want to lose you, Maisy," he whispered in her ear as he wrapped her in his warmth. "I think I'm falling in love with you," Beau added, his voice husky.

Maisy pulled back, but he didn't let her go. "That wasn't part of the plan," she said, her voice wavering, then rested her head on his chest.

"Tell me you don't feel the same way," Beau demanded, then gently lifted her chin with his fingers. She had no choice but to look at him.

"I don't…" she began, then abruptly stopped. "I can't lie," she told him. "I do have feelings for you. I know I shouldn't, but I do."

Beau didn't say another word. Instead, he leaned down and brushed his lips across hers. A shiver went down Maisy's spine.

They stood in each other's arms for what seemed an eternity. "I need to cook breakfast," Maisy said. It was madness to get involved and they both knew it. Their marriage was meant to be fake, not at all real. When all this was over, they planned an annulment. Perhaps they should stick to the plan?

And maybe their feelings were a result of the danger. They had been in each other's constant presence for days. That had to account for something. Didn't it?

Maisy pulled a large frying pan from the cupboard, then broke several eggs into it. She went to the icebox and returned with a thick slab of bacon. She cut it beautifully, considering she was out of practice, and put it on to cook.

She could feel eyes on her back, and spun around. Beau stared at her. "The moment everyone has eaten, we have to make a plan. Not only is Charlie's family at risk, but it may be our only opportunity to capture Doss."

"I know," Maisy said. "I'll be fine here."

Beau stepped toward her. "If you think I'm leaving you here alone, you can think again. My men are more than capable of handling the situation." His arms went up around her and he stared down into her face. Her expression told him a lot. "You don't think they can."

It was a statement, not a question, and Maisy immediately felt guilty. "I'm sorry, I know I should," she said, then shrugged out of his arms to tend to the food. "This is almost ready. Can you call everyone to come and eat?"

Beau frowned, then quickly left the kitchen, but was back in record time. It was clear to Maisy he wasn't prepared to leave her alone for long.

Everyone streamed into the kitchen and took a seat. She dished up the meals, and Beau delivered them. Maisy poured coffee, then finished cooking toast. A lot of toast. It was slow going, but it all disappeared quickly.

Charlie sat at the table with the others, but barely ate a bite. "Charlie," Maisy said firmly, "this is not your fault. I don't blame you one little bit."

"That's right," Beau added. "You told us the truth from the moment you arrived. I can't ask more than that. Eat up, Charlie. We need your help to pull this off."

That seemed to cheer Charlie up quite a bit, and he began to eat. He suddenly blended in so well, he almost looked like one of Beau's men.

"After everyone has eaten, we'll work out a plan of attack," Beau told everyone at the table. "We'll get one go at this, and I don't want anything to go wrong. People's lives are at stake," he said, his eyes flicking to Charlie.

Maisy felt so bad for the young bank teller. He had done nothing wrong but was caught up in Otis Doss's trail of crime. She reached across the table, and covered Charlie's hand with her own. "I truly appreciate you coming forward, Charlie," she said. "You have been a tremendous help."

He nodded, but didn't say a word. The look of relief on the young man's face was the best thing she could have wished for.

Chapter Fourteen

Beau paced the sitting room floor as they discussed how they would resolve the problem.

Otis Doss expected Charlie to return any time now, so they had to get this sorted soon. He was to report back when he'd killed Maisy. That was going to be the biggest stumbling block.

Trouble was, his family was in imminent danger. Otis Doss held them captive, just as he'd done to Maisy. Only this time, it was in their own home.

The worst part of all this was Beau's promise to Maisy. He told her he wouldn't leave her side, that he would personally protect her. Now he was itching to go with the others to see the entire scenario play out.

He couldn't leave her alone—that wasn't an option. How did Beau know Doss hadn't planned to get them all away from the house and Maisy, and attack her while they were gone? The truth was, he didn't.

Charlie handed Beau a sketch of his home. When they stormed the house, they needed to know what they were up against, and the possible hiding spots Doss might utilize. "The pantry is the obvious place," Charlie told them. "And the closet close to the front door. There's also a back door where he could easily escape." He glanced up at Beau. "Am I going to jail?" he asked quietly.

"For helping us catch Otis Doss? Not on my watch," Beau told him. "Everyone needs to familiarize themselves with the layout of the Hogan home. Memorize it, and remember every nook and cranny." They all agreed. "Here's what I believe we need to do. If you have any suggestions, don't hold back."

There were mumbles and nods of agreement as Beau outlined his plan. Everyone knew what they had to do, including the additional two men who arrived just in time for breakfast. The attack would be fast but thorough. "I don't want any casualties," Beau reiterated. "If we have to take Doss out, so be it, but I'd rather see the filthy polecat suffer for his crimes."

Everyone agreed with making the man suffer, but if he put lives at risk, they would do what was needed.

They all began to head for the door. "Wait," Beau demanded. "I'm coming with you. So I need two men to stay here with Maisy." No one volunteered. Beau knew it was because they all wanted to take Doss down and make him pay for what he'd done.

He sighed. "Flynn and Wesley, you're here with Maisy."

"Ah, boss," Flynn said, annoyed at being left behind.

"The truth is, you don't know what Doss looks like. The others do. Keep an eye on Maisy—she is determined, so don't let her out of your sight."

The two men muttered their agreement and went into the kitchen where Maisy was baking. It was something to look forward to when they returned.

~*~

As they approached the cottage, Beau reviewed the layout of the house. Each man was given his orders, and knew what to do should the plan go awry.

His team spread around the house, each keeping low so they wouldn't be seen. Beau's heart pounded. This was a life-or-death situation. Not only for Maisy, but for Charlie Hogan's entire family.

Beau's men were professionals, this is what they all did for a living. Mostly, they protected high-profile clients, but sometimes, like now, it was far more involved. Apart from wanting to take over ownership of the bank, Beau couldn't find any other motive for trying to kill Maisy. He was convinced there was more to it.

Except now was not the time. They had a job to do, and it wasn't going to be easy. They had to extradite Doss from the house without putting Charlie's family in harm's way. This would be tricky, but totally doable.

Timing was everything.

According to Charlie, and there was no reason to doubt him, Otis Doss was in possession of a derringer. Given half a chance, Beau knew the fugitive would use it. Why he still believed he could take control of the bank Beau didn't know. If he lived to be a hundred, he would never figure out the feeble minds of criminals.

"Are you ready?" he whispered to Charlie, who was white as a ghost. Beau couldn't blame him.

Charlie stared at Beau, then rolled his shoulders. "A much as I'll ever be," he said, then knocked loudly on the heavy wooden door. "Otis," he called loudly. "It's Charlie—the job is done."

Charlie glanced toward Beau, who was hidden from view. The worry on Charlie's face was palpable. When they heard a child crying, it was clear Charlie wanted to storm the house there and then. He turned to Beau again, who signaled for him to stick to the plan. Suddenly it was quiet—not a sound could be heard. Except the beating of Beau's heart.

The silence was worrying, but Beau knew from experience they had to be patient. "Don't move!" Otis yelled, barely audible through the heavy wooden door, but loud enough for Beau to hear.

Moments later, the lock clicked and the door opened wide.

As Beau had instructed him earlier, Charlie quickly stepped back out of the way. The back door was stormed at the same time as the front. Charlie's wife screamed and pulled her children close. The youngsters cried and hugged their mother. His heart broke for this young family, but he had a job to do, and he would do it.

Charlie rushed inside, but Beau was far too busy securing Doss to check on them. That would happen later.

Beau stared down at Otis Doss. Bewilderment covered his face. They achieved what they'd set out to do—all his men storming the house at once, and from different directions, meant the fool didn't know what hit him. He was surrounded and secured, along with his derringer. It was a far better result that he could have hoped for.

Sheriff Tommy Garrett stepped forward with handcuffs and secured the polecat even further. With Beau's men escorting them back to the jailhouse, there was no chance Doss would escape this time.

When he finally had the opportunity to check on Charlie's family, they were all unharmed. His wife was in her husband's arms, their young children hugging his legs. Beau was shocked to see Eva

Hogan's swollen belly—Charlie had not mentioned it, perhaps with good reason. They may not have taken the stance they did, had he known.

"It's over," Charlie told his wife, as he held her close.

She nodded, then turned to Beau. "Is my Charlie in trouble with the law?" she asked, her voice emotional, and tears swimming in her eyes. "He was protecting his family."

"Trouble? Charlie? Not at all," Beau said firmly. "The sheriff is aware of the situation, and assured me your husband will not be charged."

She slumped against her husband, and Charlie's arms tightened around her.

"We'll leave you in peace, Mrs. Hogan," Beau said, glancing at the smashed back door. "That door will be fixed within the hour, I promise," he said, then left with the remainder of his team.

When they arrived back at the mansion, Beau immediately sought out Maisy. He wrapped her in his arms and whispered, "It's all over. Doss is in custody."

"Charlie and his family? Were they harmed? Please tell me they are alright."

Beau studied her. Maisy was visibly upset. "They are perfectly fine. No one was harmed. Doss is locked up and will likely never see freedom again in his life."

"Thank you," Maisy said, tears rolling down her cheeks.

Beau wiped her tears away, then leaned down and kissed his wife like he'd never done before. Her lips were sweet as the morning dew, and soft as clouds. He couldn't imagine not having Maisy in his life, but knew he had to walk away.

He wasn't stupid enough to abandon her now, he would stay for a few days to ensure she was settled after her ordeal.

Except Beau knew it wasn't necessarily a good idea. For either of them.

Chapter Fifteen

Maisy couldn't believe how terrified she was while Beau and his men were gone. If it hadn't been for Charlie doing the right thing, she may not have survived.

Otis had taken a chance believing Charlie would do as he was told. He seemed to be of the opinion Charlie would do anything for his family. Which, in fact, he did. Going straight to Beau and telling him everything was a turning point in the entire situation.

With Otis now behind bars, everything had changed. Maisy hadn't felt this content for a very long time. Although there was still the question of whether Otis Doss had murdered her husband.

Maisy shook her head in disbelief. Beau had believed it all along, she was certain. Even though he hadn't voiced it out loud, there were hints here and there, and Maisy picked up on them. The miracle of all this was she'd come out virtually unscathed.

"What will happen now?" Maisy asked when Beau moved back and his lips no longer covered hers.

"Doss will go to trial. The belief of both myself and the sheriff is he murdered your husband."

It wasn't what Maisy was asking, and she wondered if he understood that. In the time they'd been together, she'd become far more enamored with Beau Hardner than she had a right to be. "I meant…" Her voice broke and Maisy pulled away from him. From the warmth of his arms, and from his comfort.

"I'm staying here with you." She glanced up at him and stared into Beau's eyes. Did he mean forever, or only for the night?

He frowned under her scrutiny. "You don't want me to stay?" he asked. "I thought…never mind. I'm staying for a few days, anyway."

She heard him sigh, and felt like doing the same. "Thank you," Maisy said, as though she welcomed the idea. In reality, she was concerned. Not about her safety—with Otis Doss behind bars she could breathe easy now.

Her worry was in the fact being here alone with Beau offered its own problems. Of course they were married, they had a marriage certificate to prove it. Except their marriage was only for show. Beau had no real feelings for her, even though Maisy's feelings ran deep. Telling a person you are falling in love with them was not the same as being in love.

Maisy now understood she was nothing but a show pony to Callum. A pretty wife to show off. Why she hadn't realized it sooner, she would never know, but it was now clear it's all she was. Plucked from oblivion, it should have been obvious when someone so rich wanted to marry her—a naïve young woman who didn't know better than to marry a man she barely knew.

It put her life in jeopardy, and if not for Beau, she would not be alive today.

Maisy threw herself at Beau and wrapped her arms around him. "I do want you to stay," she whispered. Except her words were so quiet, he didn't hear them.

What she really wanted to say is *I love you and never want you to leave*. Letting her heart rule her head was not the best way to go, so she held him tightly and kept her thoughts to herself.

There was a knock at the door, and Maisy reluctantly pulled away from Beau. "I'll get it," he said, and headed toward the door. Maisy watched him go, her heart breaking knowing he would be gone in a matter of days.

Gone, never to be seen again.

Except that wasn't true. He had an office in Pleasant Valley. She lived here and owned the bank as well. It would present a difficult situation for them both.

People would talk, wondering why her new husband left her so soon and applied for an annulment.

Her heart twisting in her chest, Maisy knew the gossip was the least of her worries. What she really needed to worry about was finding a way to hold on to Beau. He was her husband and she didn't want to lose him.

But did Beau feel the same way? He seemed eager to walk out of her life.

Mutterings coming from the front of the house had Maisy on alert. After everything that had happened, she wasn't surprised. What did shock her was even knowing Otis was locked up in jail, she was still afraid. Beau was right—she needed him here with her a little longer.

Forever if she could manage it. Except Maisy knew that would never happen.

The front door closed, then the man of her thoughts entered the room. "That was Bear. Charlie's home is fixed and secure again."

Maisy's breath left her body. She hadn't realized how concerned she'd been over her teller's family. "I hope they recover from their ordeal quickly," she told Beau.

He stared at her for long moments. "It will take time, but Charlie's resilient. I do worry about his wife. She is having a baby. The children are too young to understand what happened."

Trying to take it all in, Maisy stared at him. Tears welled in her eyes but Maisy fought them back. Charlie Hogan saved her life with his actions, and all she could do was fix his back door? The revelation did not sit well with Maisy. "I have to find a way to thank him. Repairing the damage we caused isn't enough. If it wasn't for me, he would not be involved in any of this." Hot tears slid down her face, and Maisy turned away.

She wasn't weak, and never had been. All of this, everything that had happened over the past weeks, it was too much. It was overwhelming, she couldn't deny it. Maisy shook her head, and turned away.

Beau reached out and enveloped her in his arms. "Today, you need to rest. Tomorrow, we will sort out the problems at the bank."

"Problems?" Maisy asked quietly. "What problems?"

"The biggest problem now is you don't have a manager, or an assistant manager. You'll have to secure an accountant as a matter of urgency." He rubbed circles on her back, and Maisy felt herself relaxing. Not enough to alleviate all her stress, but enough to feel a little better. "You need someone you can trust to ensure the books are all in order. Who knows what Otis Doss has been doing? I wouldn't be surprised if he was embezzling from the bank."

Maisy gasped. "Is…is that what this was all about? He was stealing all along? Do you think Callum knew?" Her heart pounded, and Maisy couldn't think.

"That's exactly what I think," Beau told her. He kissed her forehead, then pulled her closer still.

Maisy wished he would kiss her the way he had earlier. Not a peck on her forehead, but a real kiss on her more than willing lips. It wasn't to be. Moments later, her stomach rumbled. "I'm so sorry," she said.

Beau laughed. "How do you feel about going to the diner for supper? It can be a celebration."

"Of our marriage?" she asked, and immediately regretted it.

Gently lifting her chin with his fingers, Beau stared into her face. "Would you like it to be? I was thinking more along the lines of celebrating Doss being locked up."

Beau's expression was one of sadness. Was he as unhappy about their pending annulment as she was? Perhaps he was eager. Could she convince him not to go along with his plan? Feeling deflated, Maisy slumped against her fake husband. The man she'd come to love. He'd told her he was falling in love with her, but not once had he said he loved her.

She was fighting a losing battle, Maisy was certain. If Beau didn't love her, she might as well agree to the annulment. One loveless marriage was enough. She had no intention of spending the rest of her life wondering when he would leave her.

Chapter Sixteen

After cleaning herself up, they headed to the diner. At first, Maisy was reluctant. She glanced about, expecting Otis Doss to jump out in front of her. Beau was certain of it. "He can't get you, Maisy," he said quietly. "I'll take you to the jailhouse and prove it, if that's what it takes to make you feel better."

Why he said that, Beau wasn't sure, but Maisy needed to be reassured she was now safe. "I would like that," she told him. Her expression was wary, but it was becoming clear she needed to see for herself.

Beau changed direction, and they headed to the jailhouse. He hoped the sheriff was there, too. Otis was behind bars, but who knew what lies he would spew out trying to save his hide. It was highly possible Doss would hang for his crimes. Especially if the judge decided he had murdered Callum McGraw.

He opened the door to the jailhouse, and Sheriff Garrett sat behind his desk. Surprise covered his face.

"Maisy needed reassuring Doss is behind bars," he explained, feeling annoyed with himself for even suggesting it.

"Mrs. Hardner," the sheriff said as he stood. "Are you sure you want to do this?"

Maisy took a deep breath. She was pale, and Beau worried she would pass out. "I *need* to do it," she said firmly, then rolled her shoulders.

Beau put an arm around her for support, then led her to the cells. She stood staring at the man Callum McGraw once considered a friend. The man who had waited until the right moment to make his move. Her whole body trembled.

"Doss!" the sheriff shouted. "Get up, you lazy sod!"

Doss was lying on the bed, but now stood. Maisy stared at him for long moments, then turned away. "I've seen enough. I'm ready to go," she said, then spun around to face him again. "Did you murder my husband?" she suddenly demanded. Fury covered her face, and Beau knew she meant business.

For a while, it appeared the prisoner had no intention of answering. Hands on her hips, Maisy demanded an answer. "Well? I'm waiting?" she snapped. It was all Beau could do not to laugh. Except it wasn't a laughing matter.

"You realize it won't make a difference to your sentence," Sheriff Tommy Garrett said. "Give the lady some closure on her late husband's death."

Doss stared at his feet. "I poisoned his coffee." His words were matter-of-fact, as though he was simply passing the time of day with polite conversation. It confirmed Beau's long-held belief Otis Doss was a cold-blooded killer.

"Why? Why would you do that?" Maisy asked, her voice breaking. "Callum considered you a friend." Beau reached for her hand. She needed answers.

"He began checking the ledgers. When he discovered I'd embezzled money, he threatened to call the sheriff. I couldn't let that happen."

"So you killed him," Maisy said, then spun around and hurried out of the sheriff's office and into the fresh air.

Beau couldn't be more relieved at the revelations if he tried.

~*~

Standing outside in the fresh air was bliss. Beau needed it as much as Maisy did. If he hadn't heard it with his own ears, Beau would never believe Doss had confessed to murder. He turned at the click of the door behind him.

"That's a relief," Tommy Garrett said. "I did get more information on Doss, and it was enlightening." He held a piece of paper, and handed it over to Beau.

He scanned the page, then relayed the information to Maisy. "Otis Doss was a wanted man. He was accused of embezzlement at the Helena Bank some years ago. Once confronted, he disappeared. There was also a case of poisoning that didn't go to plan. He'd only used enough poison to make the person very ill. They had a lucky escape."

Maisy lost all color in her face.

"That was truly brave of you, confronting Doss like that," Sheriff Garrett said. Beau handed the paper back to him. "We can use that confession in his trial. I may need to call you two as witnesses."

Maisy straightened her shoulders. "Whatever it takes," she said firmly. She turned to Beau. "I'm hungry. Can we eat now?" she said, then headed toward the diner without waiting for a response.

His wife was far more feisty than any other women he'd known. It was another thing that made him love her.

~*~

"The meal was scrumptious," Maisy said as she dabbed at her lips with a napkin. "I didn't realize how hungry I was."

Beau couldn't help but grin. "Your rumbling stomach should have been enough proof."

She glared at him, then sipped the delicious lemonade the diner was famous for. "What are we going to do about the ledgers," she asked Beau, totally ignoring his comment. "Disregard them as though nothing ever happened?"

That certainly would be the easy way out, but it was not an option. "The sheriff will need evidence of embezzlement for the trial, despite the confession. Charlie might know an accountant we can trust. We can talk to him tomorrow."

They finished up their beverages and then left. The sun was setting and the sky was lit with a mixture of pinks, yellows, and blue. It was a beautiful way to end the day. Especially after the harsh times Maisy had endured recently.

Beau offered his arm, and Maisy accepted. "It is so pretty out here now." She looked far more relaxed than she had since the day he met her—with very good reason. Her kidnapper was now safely locked away behind bars. Goodness knew how long it would take for the trial to be held. It would be dependent on when a judge was available.

Leading her toward a wooden bench, Beau indicated for Maisy to sit down. "I thought it would be nice to sit and watch the sunset," he said, then stared into her face. His heart pounded at the thought of losing her. How he had let himself fall in love with a client, Beau would never know. Except he did know—it was easy to fall in love with Maisy. She was beautiful, forceful, and determined. She knew her mind, and didn't let anyone sway her from what she wanted to do.

The very thought had him smiling.

"Thank you for everything," Maisy said, as she continued to gaze at the setting sun. "I can never thank you and your men enough."

"We were simply doing our job," Beau lied. He had never gone to such lengths for a client as he had for Maisy. The thought of applying for an annulment had his heart twisting so much it hurt.

She turned to stare at him. "I don't believe you," Maisy said matter-of-factly.

In that moment, Beau knew he should confess his love for her. Except it was the last thing he should do, and Beau knew it. Maisy had to be left to live her life the way she wanted. Their agreement was for them to part ways once she was safe again. Since Doss was now in jail, and would stay there, she was safe.

"About the annulment," she said out of the blue as she stared down into her hands. "I…"

Beau's heart thudded. This wasn't what he wanted to hear. "I'll arrange for the paperwork tomorrow.

It will take time for it to come through." That was that. Maisy had made it perfectly clear she wanted to part ways with him.

She continued to stare down at her hands, then without notice stood. "I want to go home now," she told him firmly. Beau stood and offered his arm again. Maisy hurried ahead.

How would he live the rest of his life without Maisy in it? Beau now knew he had no choice.

Chapter Seventeen

It was all Maisy could do not to cry. When Beau said he would apply for their annulment tomorrow, her heart shattered. The last thing she wanted was for Beau to leave her. She might not have been widowed long, but her first marriage was not filled with love. Far from it.

Maisy would rather forget it altogether.

She had received far more affection from Beau during this tumultuous period than she had in the six months she was married to Callum McGraw.

How she would continue without Beau she didn't know. He was everything she wanted in a husband, despite being a virtual stranger.

Correction, after six months married to Callum, she hadn't known him as well as she knew Beau.

As much as she hated Otis Doss for what he'd done, if it hadn't been for him, she would never have met Beau. Experiencing his affection, even for such a short time, was better than not knowing him at all.

The worst of it was having to see him around town, and not having him in her life.

As they arrived at the mansion, he pulled out the key and opened the door. He glanced about as though still worried about her safety. "Am I still in danger?" she asked bluntly.

He studied her, then stepped back. "I don't believe so. Doss was working alone. At least we believe he was."

That didn't reassure her. Her legs felt like jelly. Maisy believed the danger to be over. Now she found out there was a possibility it may not be. "It is safe or not?" she demanded. Beau's lips quirked upward, which annoyed her greatly.

"It's safe," he said firmly.

"I'm going to bed," Maisy said, and headed toward her dressing room. He waited outside, then when she went to her bedroom, Beau followed her there. "What are you doing in here?" she demanded. "At your own admission, you do not need to protect me anymore." Her heart fluttered. Having Beau in her bedroom for reasons other than protection had her thinking all sorts of things. Her mind was going to places it had no right to even imagine.

She stared up at him as Beau moved closer. The fluttering of her heart turned to pounding. She couldn't think straight with her fake husband so close to her. His arms came up around her, and then he kissed her.

It was wrong. Completely wrong. They had vowed to get an annulment, yet here he was, in her bedroom, trying to seduce her. Maisy suddenly pulled back. "What are you doing?" she whispered.

Beau stared into her eyes. His expression showed the pain he was feeling. Instead of answering, he leaned down to kiss her again. Maisy was fully aware she only wore her nightgown, and was completely vulnerable to this man who had worked his way into her heart.

She put her hands to his chest and pushed him away. "I can't do this," she said quietly but firmly. "Once the annulment goes through, we will no longer be married."

"Is that what you want?" he asked. "An annulment? I thought we were getting along fine." His arms enveloped her again, and Maisy slumped against him.

"I'm not sure what I want," she said truthfully. "Perhaps you should sleep in the spare room tonight."

He shook his head at her suggestion. "I am staying in here with you." He glanced toward the armchair sitting in the corner of the room. "I'll take the chair," he said, then sighed.

As much as she wanted Beau to be her real husband, until a decision was made about their future, she would keep her distance. Maisy hoped Beau would do the same.

~*~

Beau accompanied Maisy to the bank the next morning. He still had security there, although she wasn't sure why. With Otis Doss locked up in jail, the danger was over. Wasn't it?

The moment they entered, he headed straight for Charlie Hogan. Maisy was surprised to see him there, after everything Charlie and his family had endured the day before. "Charlie," Beau said. "If you have a moment, I need to talk to you."

Charlie stared at him momentarily, then went pale.

"Nothing to worry about," Beau assured him. "Maisy and I need your help."

The two men went upstairs to what used to be Callum's meeting room, and Maisy followed. She already knew the nature of the discussion and wanted to be privy to the information.

When the three were comfortably seated, Beau turned to Charlie. "We need your help, Charlie," Beau said. "We…Maisy, is in need of a good accountant. Do you know anyone trustworthy?"

Charlie fidgeted about in his seat for a matter of seconds, then ran a hand through his hair. "That would be me," he finally said. "I was the bank's accountant until Otis came along. Then suddenly I was demoted to clerk."

Maisy gasped, and Beau frowned. Reaching for her hand, Beau squeezed it, trying to reassure her. Callum had left a total mess behind him. It made Maisy wonder exactly what he'd been up to.

"Were you given a reason?" Beau asked, still holding her hand. The revelations were disturbing.

"Not at all," Charlie said. "But I'd noticed some discrepancies in the ledgers. I told Callum, but figured he was the one causing it. Within days, Otis arrived and took over."

Beau stared at Maisy. It was all becoming clear now. Otis was there to help cover Callum's tracks, but instead, continued the embezzlement for his own benefit. Maisy was shocked at the revelations, but knew she shouldn't be. She turned to Beau and nodded. They had anticipated what to do if the situation arose.

"Charlie," Beau said firmly. "Maisy wants you to take over as bank accountant again." Beau ran a hand across his chin. "You'll be known as the bank manager." It was Charlie's turn to gasp.

"There will be a substantial pay increase, of course," Maisy added. "What do you say, Charlie? Do you accept, or do you need time to think about it?"

"Oh, I definitely accept," Charlie said, a wide grin on his face.

Maisy couldn't help but breathe a sigh of relief.

Chapter Eighteen

Now the bank's problems were sorted, Beau knew his time with Maisy was limited. They still had to find a trustworthy replacement for Charlie's former teller position, but that should be an easy task.

He could already tell a weight had been lifted from her shoulders—her face was more relaxed, and she was even smiling from time to time. What Callum McGraw had done to Maisy was apprehensible. It was clear her former husband did not value Maisy the way Beau did.

Perhaps she was correct when she said Callum had never loved her. He couldn't even imagine what her life must have been like with him. Beau guessed he only married her to give his position at the bank some legitimacy. It had to have been a difficult situation for her.

He stood, then helped Maisy to her feet. Charlie followed suit. "This is your office now," Beau told Charlie, as he pointed toward the manager's office. "Feel free to change the furniture around if you wish."

"You'll need an assistant—we can talk about that later," Maisy told him. "Settle in today, and we'll discuss getting more staff. Tomorrow perhaps? You'll need a replacement for your former position, too."

Charlie shook his head. Beau was certain it was in disbelief. Maisy had wanted to reward Charlie in some way for saving her life, but wasn't sure how. This has worked out perfectly.

Beau moved closer to Maisy. "We should go," he said. "We have much to do." The one thing Maisy wanted was the one thing Beau dreaded. He'd promised to apply for an annulment the moment the danger was over. Except he'd said it before he'd fallen in love with her, and now he was trapped. Beau had always been a man of his word, and needed to carry out his agreement.

Even if it meant shattering his heart in the process.

Walking downstairs with Maisy was difficult. Knowing this would likely be the last time he would stand by her side as her husband tore him apart. He spoke to his men and explained Charlie was taking over as manager, then the pair left together.

He barely managed to put one foot in front of the other, but he did. When they reached the church, Maisy stopped abruptly. He turned to face her. She was deathly white, and Beau couldn't fathom why.

Her eyes closed, she whispered, the words barely audible. "I… I can't," she began. She opened her eyes, and without warning, ran toward home.

Beau had no choice but to follow her.

It didn't take long to catch up with Maisy. The house wasn't far from the church. It wasn't far from anything. She was trying to unlock the front door when he arrived. Wrapping his hand around hers, he took the key out of her shaking hand. "Let me do that," he offered. She didn't refuse.

It felt good to have her in his arms, although technically, he was standing behind her, not hugging Maisy. It was obvious she was upset. The reason had eluded him.

The moment the door was open, she hurried inside. Beau followed her, still confused about her motives. "Maisy," he said gently, "talk to me."

She turned and shook her head.

He was more confused than ever. "You know Otis Doss cannot harm you? He is locked up, and I doubt he'll ever see freedom again. Especially now we know the truth from Charlie."

She took a shuddering breath. "It's not that," Maisy said quietly, then sat on the sofa.

Beau sat next to her. "Then what is the problem?" He was becoming concerned. Had the stress of the situation finally tipped her over the edge of sanity? Maisy turned to face him. Her eyes were brimming with tears. "Oh, Maisy," he said, then scurried across until he was as close to her as he could get.

She leaned her head on his shoulder, and her tears ran down her cheeks and onto his shirt. His heart was breaking. If only he understood, then perhaps he could help.

"I don't want to lose you," she whispered as he wiped her tears away.

Beau's hand paused. Did she really say what he thought he heard? "Are you saying…?" Did he dare believe his ears? He twisted around until he could stare into her face. Her tear-streaked face. "I love you, Maisy," he said. "The last thing I want is to lose you."

"I love you, too," she whispered. Beau leaned in and kissed her gently. His heart pounding, he pulled her closer, then kissed Maisy the way a husband should kiss his wife.

~*~

Two months later…

The circuit judge arrived for the trial of Otis Doss. According to the sheriff, it was an open-and-closed case. With the testimony from Charlie Hogan, and the falsified ledgers as proof, Doss was charged with several offenses including murder, attempted murder, stalking, and four counts of kidnapping and embezzlement.

Maisy was called to the stand for her statement regarding her kidnapping. Beau was heartbroken listening to the things Doss had done to her while he had her locked up. No wonder she'd been on edge. The biggest surprise was she'd been able to escape.

Beau was called to give his version of her escape and Doss's stalking. He also spoke about Charlie Hogan and how he had saved Maisy's life.

Otis Doss sat in the dock, his expression one of fury. The judge adjourned the case until the afternoon to allow him to read through all the evidence provided. Surely, he had enough evidence already to sentence the polecat? The fact he couldn't make a decision worried Beau. And Maisy.

"He's going to get off, isn't he?" she asked as they walked out of the makeshift courtroom.

Beau put his arm around her shoulders. "I can't see how he can, but perhaps there is new information that's come to light. Let's eat. You might feel better then."

She shook her head. "We can eat, but I won't feel better until he is locked up for the rest of his life."

They headed to the diner, and were joined by two of Beau's men, Bear and Cole, along with Sheriff Tommy Garrett. Maisy picked at her food, and Beau didn't blame her. It was a stressful day. The weeks of waiting for the trial was hard enough for her, but to have to wait another couple of hours must be excruciating. Especially when they all believed it would be a cut and dry case.

It seemed like forever before the sheriff announced it was time to return to the courtroom. Beau stood and helped Maisy to her feet. She was shaking uncontrollably. He put an arm around her, and held her close, then guided her to the courthouse and into her seat.

"All rise," the sheriff told those who had assembled to hear the verdict. The judge took his seat. "Be seated," Tommy told the room.

"I've reviewed new evidence that has come to light," Judge Hannigan said, waving a sheet of paper for all to see. "This information outlines Otis Doss's repeated offenses in a variety of towns over a number of years. Callum McGraw was not his first murder victim, but he will be his last." The judge turned to face Doss. "Otis Doss, I sentence you to hanging. You will not ruin any more lives." He pounded his gavel, then stood. Those in the gallery also stood. Beau turned to Maisy who was far more pale than he liked.

Without warning, she slumped to the floor. He was there to catch her, as he would be for the rest of her life.

Epilogue

Four years later…

Maisy stared at the scene before her, from where she stood on the porch. She couldn't believe the happiness she felt with Beau as her husband. He was a caring man, well beyond what she could ever have anticipated. Her expectations were tainted by her short marriage to Callum McGraw.

It made her wonder if Beau was ensuring she didn't go down a similar path. She shook her head—it was a silly notion. Her husband was being himself. He was a wonderful husband, and an amazing father.

"Mama," three-year-old Isaac called. "Look, no hands!" he said, as he sat atop the pony he was learning to ride.

Beau quickly intervened. "Hold on or I'll take you off," his father told the boy firmly. It was evident he was going to be like his father. Hard-headed and determined.

It was only moments later baby Rosa cried. Maisy went to her room, her heart filled with love. With everything that happened four years ago, they decided not to live in the mansion. Instead, it was turned into a boarding house. They installed a manager, who ran the place to their satisfaction.

They'd bought a small ranch. Somewhere special to raise their brood of children, and teach them about the outdoors. Not to mention how to be the best people they could be. Maisy loved it here—it was serene, and the fresh air did them all good.

It wasn't like they needed the money. Charlie ran the bank like clockwork, and Maisy trusted him implicitly. Charlie and his wife, Eva, were expecting their fifth child. Maisy glanced down at her swollen belly and smiled.

Maisy was overcome with emotion. She adored her expanding family, and loved her life with Beau. It made her wonder what her life would be like right now had Callum lived. More than likely, she would have left him by now. After all, a loveless marriage was not what she'd agreed to.

She lifted Rosa out of her crib, then changed her wet diaper. It was then she heard the front door open, then close. Scurrying feet had Isaac arriving by her side moments later, followed by his father. "Baby Rosa," Isaac said, then leaned in to hug his baby sister. The scene before her warmed Maisy's heart.

Beau came to stand beside Maisy, and put an arm around her. "I love you so much," he said, then moved in to kiss her cheek.

Turning her head at just the right time ensured he kissed her lips instead. It was the way she liked it. "I love you too," Maisy said, then felt young Isacc tugging on her skirt. Beau lifted him up and the little family all hugged together. One of Maisy's favorite things to do.

"Love you, too," their son said. Moments later, their unborn baby kicked, and Isaac laughed.

Maisy understood how blessed she and Beau were. They had the perfect place to live, a loving family, and their faith.

What more could she ask for?

From the Author

Thank you so much for reading my book – I hope you enjoyed it.

I would greatly appreciate you leaving a review where you purchased, even if it is only a one-liner. It helps to have my books more visible!

About the Author

Multi-published, award-winning and bestselling author Cheryl Wright, former secretary, debt collector, account manager, writing coach, and shopping tour hostess, loves reading.

She writes both historical and contemporary western romance, as well as romantic suspense.

She lives in Melbourne, Australia, and is married with two adult children and has six grandchildren, and twin great-grandchildren.

When she's not writing, she can be found in her craft room making greeting cards.

Links

Website: *http://www.cheryl-wright.com/*

Facebook Reader Group:
https://www.facebook.com/groups/cherylwrightauthor/

Join My Newsletter:

https://cheryl-wright.com/newsletter/
(and receive a free book)